A TAIL OF MURDER

A WILDWOOD WITCH MYSTERY: BOOK 1

ELLE ADAMS

To be notified when Elle Adams's next book is released, sign up to her author newsletter.

"We're home!"

As soon as I'd jumped off my broomstick, Tansy, my squirrel familiar, raced ahead to the summit of the hill and looked out on the town of Wildwood Heath. I followed at a slower pace, finding it a little hard to summon up any enthusiasm. Yes, the scenery was as pristine as ever, as if the sun shone a little brighter upon its vibrant green fields and verdant woodlands than it did anywhere else, but the sheer amount of broomstick traffic criss-crossing the skies above our heads brought a dark cloud which reminded me of my real reason for being here.

Even on the day of the Head Witch's funeral, Wildwood Heath didn't look like a town mourning its most beloved coven leader. The enclave held the title of the Midlands' most popular magical tourist spot for wildlife lovers and nature, in addition to its high ranking in several regional sporting championships. Wildwood

Heath—and the coven which gave the town its name—played to win.

A flock of broomsticks zoomed overhead, nearly blowing Tansy head over heels downhill. She scurried back to my side, tail fur in disarray and eyes bright with excitement. "I bet there are witches from all over the country flying in."

"They're supposed to be here for a funeral, not the regional Sky Hopper championship." I positioned my broom over my shoulder to avoid it being swept away in the breeze kicked up by the new arrivals as I walked downhill towards one of the forested paths leading into the town. With a little luck, I'd be able to get undercover before I ran into the press.

I should have known better than to tempt fate. No sooner had I entered the woodland than the flash of a camera dazzled my eyes, and a witch and wizard in identical red cloaks and hats leapt out of the bushes. The wizard held the camera while the witch waved a microphone in front of my face. Tansy, typically, climbed up my shoulder and hid herself behind my hair.

"Hello, there!" the witch said. "We're Clarice and Speck from the *Blue Moon,* and we're looking to interview some out-of-town witches and wizards for our segment on the funeral of the former Head Witch."

"Good for you." I knew better than to offer a single word to the region's most notorious magical tabloid newspaper. A fair proportion of its most sensational and ridiculous stories over the past few decades had centred on my family—or more specifically, my grandmother. Grandma had had the last laugh, though, clinging tenaciously to her position of Head Witch until the moment she'd died peacefully in her sleep last week.

Unconcerned by my rebuff, Clarice tailed me down the path through the woodland, microphone hand outstretched. "You're going to the funeral, aren't you? What was your relationship to the Head Witch?"

Long-suffering granddaughter, I thought.

Behind me, Tansy jumped off my shoulder to chase one of the local squirrels out of a tree.

Speck came to such a sudden halt that he almost dropped his camera. "It can't be."

Clarice's gaze followed my familiar, and then understanding crossed her face. Uh-oh. I beckoned Tansy to come over to me, and she scurried protectively up my leg as I quickened my pace.

"Want me to stop them?" she whispered in my ear.

"Please," I breathed. "We need to drive them away before they reach the coven's territory."

"Wait!" Clarice cried. "The Head Witch's granddaughter has a red squirrel familiar, doesn't she? You must be Robin Wildwood."

I tried not to cringe at the mention of my name, but it'd been unrealistic to expect to fly under the radar for long. Everyone had to come to the funeral of the former coven leader and Head Witch of the region. Even her estranged granddaughter, whose magic was good for only one thing… havoc.

Luckily, havoc was precisely what the *Blue Moon*'s reporters deserved. While Tansy scurried back down my arm with a flick of her bushy tail, I whispered a quick spell under my breath, directed towards the birds nesting in the nearby trees.

Clarice and Speck leapt back with cries of surprise when a flurry of birds descended in a sweep of falling leaves. While they scrambled to protect their precious recording equipment from the aerial onslaught, I took the opportunity to disappear among the trees. I had to use my broomstick to whack some low-hanging branches out of the way, but at least the thick trees hid me from view. Even in the most tangled part of the woods, it wasn't hard to spot Tansy's bright tail bobbing in the air as she leapt from one branch to the next until we reached the boundary of Wildwood Coven territory.

If I knew Mum, she'd expressly forbidden the press from setting foot anywhere near the house, so I exhaled in a sigh of relief as I left the thicket behind.

Then Tansy's tail began to wag furiously. Too late, I spotted the spiky outline of a hedgehog sitting on the path in front of us. The little hedgehog was the size of my palm, but the recrimination in his beady eyes made dread twist inside me, especially when I remembered the tell-tale green glow around my hands from the magic I'd used against those reporters.

"You're late," said the hedgehog, who happened to be called Prickles. He also bore a startling resemblance to his owner, my brother Ramsey. Not that either of them appreciated me pointing that out.

"They didn't move the funeral three hours earlier, did they?" I asked. "Because I checked the time on the email a dozen times in the last day."

Instead of answering, Prickles gave a sniff. "Your mother wants to meet with you."

"How on earth did she know I was here?" My plain old bog-standard broomstick wasn't *that* distinctive, while my familiar's bright, bushy tail wouldn't have been visible to her unless she'd been watching the sky through a pair of binoculars for the past few hours. Surely the future Head Witch and leader of the Wildwood Coven had more important things to do with her time than to spy on her estranged daughter. Like organising a funeral, for instance.

"She sensed your arrival, of course," said Prickles. "She's the coven leader, or she will be."

"So she hasn't taken the position yet."

Reading between the lines, she was also still mad at me for skipping out on the last few family gatherings. As was Ramsey, if he'd sent his familiar to reprimand me instead of coming in person. Admittedly, he must have his hands full if he'd volunteered to help Mum with the funeral arrangements as well as being head of Wildwood Heath's law enforcement. He was the youngest-ever wizard to take the title, as I'd been repeatedly reminded during the last family gathering I'd attended. As if I needed to be told that one of us was the family's pride and joy while the other… well, I was currently being lectured by a hedgehog. You can work out the rest for yourself.

Prickles gave me a stern look. "No, but there's a tight schedule, and your mother would dearly prefer it if you didn't go wandering off on any detours."

"I only detoured through the forest to avoid the press," I told him. "They're ambushing people from the bushes. Does Mum know?"

"She can't keep them away from the town altogether," said Prickles. "This is a historic occasion."

No kidding. The passing of the leader of one of the region's major witch covens would qualify as front-page news in the paranormal world, especially one who'd also happened to be a Head Witch. Anyone could lead a coven, but each Head Witch had attained the very pinnacle of what a witch could achieve. Already, speculation had flooded the Wizarding Web as to who would be chosen as her replacement, but while covens picked their leaders via a voting process, selecting a new Head Witch was... complicated. Even my control-freak mother wouldn't be able to guarantee being chosen.

I'd long since resigned myself to her being even less compromising than usual, but my apprehension built when I followed Prickles along the path which led along the back of the houses owned by the more prominent members of the Wildwood Coven. As soon as we came into view of the wide expanse of lawn at the back of Aunt Shannon's house, Tansy ran off in pursuit of the magpie sitting on the fence: my aunt's familiar, Myrtle. The bird took flight with a shriek and a scattering of feathers, while Prickles shook his little head. "She'd better not wreck your mother's roses."

"She'll be on her best behaviour." Another magpie feather came drifting down onto the path. "Besides, you know that magpie was probably spying on you, don't you?"

Myrtle was as bad as those reporters for poking her beak into people's business and taking the gossip back to her owner. I'd frequently had to send Tansy to turf the magpie out of bushes and off windowsills where she'd been eavesdropping, and I'd bet she had both eyes open for trouble on the day of the funeral.

While my familiar ran free to her heart's content, I followed Prickles past Aunt Shannon's lawns to the equally large garden next door, where carefully arranged beds of flowers surrounded a large greenhouse housing the herbs and plants Mum needed for her spells. I recognised Piper's handiwork and hoped I might run into my oldest friend, the coven's gardener, but it wasn't until I'd reached the whitewashed walls of the house itself that I spotted a blond witch wearing casual clothing which rendered her almost unrecognisable at first. Then my heart did a flying leap into my throat. *Oh, boy.* I could count on one hand the number of times I'd seen Mum in a T-shirt and muddy jeans, and most of those had been when I was a toddler. To see her snipping away at the rosebush with a pair of gardening tools was jarring, while the petals littering the path looked alarmingly like droplets of blood. Was she still mad at me? Given that she had to have spotted me by now, I'd have said yes, she was.

Her familiar acknowledged me first. Horace, a ginger-and-white cat with an orange tuft on his tail which had caused me to occasionally get him confused with Tansy when I was a kid—usually with disastrous results—looked at me haughtily. "Where's that squirrel of yours?"

"There." I pointed over the fence to the bright-red shape of Tansy running along the top of the fence. "Mother, it's me."

"Robin." She didn't take her eyes off the rosebush she was pruning. "So you finally showed your face, did you?"

"I'm sorry about Grandma."

"No, you aren't."

So much for starting out on the right foot. "I am. She ought to have retired before she worked herself to death."

"You know that wasn't her style." Mum finally turned around. "You're looking awfully windswept."

Speak for yourself. Her hair was twisted into a topknot and hardly looked better than my own wild blond curls, while mud stained her pale hands. The steely expression in her green eyes dared me to point it out. Angry and grieving or not, she was still the future coven leader. "That's because I flew here and ran into a bunch of reporters."

She muttered something uncomplimentary under her breath. "I hope you didn't embarrass us."

"I didn't." Technically, the stunt I'd pulled with the birds had been more humiliating for them than it'd been for me. "They're not allowed to come to the funeral, are they?"

"Certainly not." More red petals scattered onto the grass. "Any reporter who sets foot on Wildwood Coven territory will spend the rest of the week as a rat."

"Tansy would like that." I glimpsed her running across the lawn before she ascended one of the bird feeders and attempted to pry it open.

Mum tutted. "I forgot how wily she is."

"She's a red squirrel. She has to be."

Tansy took pride in being the only red squirrel familiar in town, and while the pair of us shared a similar temperament, squirrels were easier to forgive for being arbiters of chaos.

Mum turned back to the roses. "The funeral is at dusk, but we'll have to be there an hour earlier to welcome the guests."

"I know. Rowan told me."

Her jaw twitched. "You spoke to your cousin, then."

"Yes, on the phone. She told me the news." I'd always been closer to my youngest cousin than I had to the rest of the family, but with Aunt Shannon being Mum's main rival for the title of Head Witch, I should have guessed she wouldn't appreciate the reminder that I'd contacted her daughter before the rest of the family.

"Did she now?" said Mum. "Are you sure she wasn't fishing for information to pass on to her mother?"

"It's not as if Aunt Shannon has any reason to be interested in my life." I might also have pointed out that Mum and I had barely been speaking to one another at the time, but I didn't. "Besides, if she hadn't told me about the funeral when she did, I might not have been able to book the week off work."

"Work," she repeated. "Stacking shelves, is it?"

Heat crept up my neck. "Deliveries. I'm saving for—"

"Deliveries?" she repeated. "Don't they use magic for that these days?"

"I'm a courier for private clients." In other words, I delivered boxes of priceless magical junk to rich witches and wizards and ensured said artefacts arrived in one piece. The work paid a pittance compared to how much our clients actually earned, but I liked travelling to new places, and it was a mile better than living under the watchful eyes of the Wildwood Coven.

"I thought you said you wanted to be a photographer."

"I need to save for a decent camera first." At the moment, most of my salary went towards rent. Mum had offered to keep giving me an allowance but only if I stayed here in Wildwood Heath and worked for the coven. I'd told her point-blank that I didn't need or want bribery, and it was far more satisfying to pay my own way, even if it took longer.

"Based on the average magical courier's salary, that'll take you about a decade, won't it?"

Thanks for that, Mum. "I'm waiting for a promotion."

"Always a contrarian." She shook her head. "Even as a toddler, you'd insist you wanted the opposite of what you did, solely for the sake of an argument."

"This isn't the same as that time I wanted to eat a mud pie as a two-year-old, Mother."

Admittedly, this was my third attempt to make it alone since I'd left home at eighteen, and the previous two had ended with me returning to Wildwood Heath with my tail between my legs. While Mum had raised Ramsey and me more or less single-handedly since she'd divorced our father, she'd balked at the idea of me removing myself from the rest of the family and had barely spoken to me since I'd moved away again three years prior.

Mum and I had never seen eye to eye—possibly because she was a foot taller than me and had a tendency to look right over my head as though someone far more interesting stood over my shoulder. Like my brother, for instance. When her attention skimmed past me, I rotated on my heel and saw Ramsey approaching us. My brother was already dressed in his smartest suit, his blond curls tamed flat against his head, and the sight of Prickles sitting on his shoulder would have been an oddity if not for the fact that their haughty expressions were mirror images of each other.

Ramsey halted in front of me, his own gaze fixed somewhere behind me. Why he'd inherited Mum's height and I hadn't was as much a mystery as why he'd inherited the brains and I'd just got the temper.

"Did you know your familiar is running amok around the garden?" he asked me.

"Nice to see you too." I straightened upright to look him in the eyes. "Tansy had to endure the indignity of flying on a broom, so I thought I'd let her stretch her legs for a bit."

In truth, my familiar took instructions as well as I had as an apprentice witch, which was to say that my commands went in one furry ear and out the other one most of the time. I didn't mind, but there was nothing like being around family to make me feel like I was being forced back into the shoes I'd once worn as a kid, which pinched my feet with every step and made me hobble with discomfort. Metaphorically speaking.

My brother did not look convinced. "Did you at least pack appropriate clothing for a funeral?"

"Sure." Nobody would notice I was wearing my Pikachu socks if I wore my longest cloak, would they? "I just need to change, but we have plenty of time."

"We most certainly do not," said Mum. "My sister will be here at least an hour early."

"So you're pruning roses… why?"

She huffed and turned back to the flowerbed. "Because I was waiting for you to arrive."

"All right." I held up my hands in an attempt to placate her. "You didn't throw out my stuff, did you?"

"No, I didn't," she said. "You should be glad of it, since you took off without so much as a word of goodbye."

Ramsey winced, while I watched the back of her blond head. "You weren't around the morning I left. I looked everywhere."

It wasn't like she hadn't known I was leaving that day,

but the building tension over my last weeks in town had culminated in one of our worst arguments the night before, and since we shared the same stubbornness, neither of us had been willing to give ground.

Mum turned back to face me. "You'd be much closer to your goals if you'd taken your grandmother up on her offer."

Not this again. "She didn't actually want me to work as her assistant. I guarantee I wouldn't have lasted a week before she'd kicked me out of the office."

"If you'd given it a try—"

"I did. Don't you remember?"

Back as a fledgeling witch, I'd had a brief stint helping out at one of the many Head Witch ceremonies with some of the other witches from the academy. Grandma had requested that we conjure up a stream of live birds to form the words "Head Witch" in the air. Unfortunately, I'd jumbled all the letters, and then the birds had refused to leave me alone, cawing and hooting and leaving droppings everywhere throughout the rest of the ceremony.

Shockingly, I'd been left off the list at the next ceremony and at every one since. The memory alone brought a flush to my face as bright as Tansy's tail.

"You're not a child any longer," she said. "Besides, this week's ceremony will be the first one where the leadership of the coven is guaranteed to change hands. It'll be good practise for when your own turn comes."

My heart sank. So she was still dead set on me eventually leading the coven… and, therefore, Wildwood Heath itself. Despite the process being democratic on paper, the coven leadership was traditionally inherited through matriarchal lines, and almost nobody dared to rock the boat by voting for an outsider. As the oldest daughter, Mum naturally expected to take over from Grandma, and since she'd refused point-blank to remarry or have any more kids, that meant all eyes would be on me next. While Ramsey was the eldest, and we'd hardly be the only coven to be led by a wizard rather than a witch, he'd decided to go into magical law enforcement instead and left me as the only possible contender.

Somehow, the notion of asking me what I actually wanted for my future was not on anyone's radar.

Luckily—or not—Tansy decided to interrupt at that moment by executing a flying leap onto the bird feeder, sending startled blackbirds fluttering everywhere.

Mum sighed. "Take that familiar of yours indoors and get ready for the funeral."

This is going to go well.

2

I fidgeted in my seat, wishing I'd bought a new hat for the funeral. The back of my head itched so much that I was starting to get concerned that I'd accidentally brought along the nest of spiders I'd disturbed when I'd dug it out of the back of the wardrobe in my childhood bedroom. I hadn't worn a proper pointed hat in years, but as promised, I'd dressed in the traditional coven attire, which hadn't changed in at least a couple of centuries. If you didn't count my Pikachu socks, anyway, which weren't visible under the long cloak that swept down to my feet.

My brother sat on my other side, so still that he looked like someone had cast a freeze-frame spell on him. From the occasional huff of disapproval he sent in my direction, he was tempted to do exactly that to me. I couldn't be the only one who'd started to get bored with the proceedings, surely. Mum and Aunt Shannon had already had their turn to speak, and it seemed every single person crammed into the room had something to say about the former

Head Witch. Her former assistant, Stacy, had been on the stage for at least twenty minutes, her whiny voice droning on, while false-sounding sobs punctuated her words. I might have felt sorry for her given that she was now out of a job, but if her speech went on for much longer, I'd be tempted to direct Tansy to crawl up her leg and put a stop to her before someone else dropped dead from sheer boredom.

Tansy, lucky thing, got free rein to explore the gardens to her heart's content while the rest of us were crammed into this room. Half the town was in attendance, and dozens more people had come from other magical communities to pay their respects. And, it seemed, give speeches. With two exceptions: the press and yours truly. Nobody had asked me for a contribution. I also didn't yet know the contents of Grandma's will, though the tradition was to wait a few days after the death of a Head Witch in case her ghost came back to challenge her living self's words.

If Grandma's ghost had made an appearance today, it'd inject some excitement into the proceedings, but no such luck. Her burnished coffin at the front of the room, decked out in bright flowers, remained solemn and still as the speeches finally came to an end. Mum then returned to the stage—wearing her own dark cloak and hat, without any mud or gardening tools in sight—and gave the concluding speech.

"That should have been me," Aunt Shannon said in a carrying whisper from my brother's other side. "The Head Witch wanted me to do the final speech."

Mum ignored her. "Thank you for attending. Please proceed out of the hall and into the garden."

In unison, we rose to our feet and left the hall with Mum and Aunt Shannon leading the way. It must have taken a herculean effort for them not to immediately snap into an argument, and the palpable tension between them crackled like electricity in the air while Ramsey and I followed them outside. As kids, Aunt Shannon and Mum had been as fiercely competitive as my brother and me. The difference was that Mum always won.

The paved area behind the coven's headquarters stretched out before us, containing tables laden with refreshments and a handful of individuals who hadn't been invited to the funeral but had decided to show up anyway. I didn't spot any cameras among them, thankfully. While they weren't technically allowed to sneak in without an invitation, the coven's headquarters was open to any witch or wizard, and it had no official owner until the next coven leader was crowned.

Behind me, the rest of the funeral's attendees spilled out into the garden, and Mum was already surrounded by so many people that I had no trouble avoiding her gaze. I didn't see Dad among the attendees, but his partner, a werewolf named Jessica, wasn't on the guest list, so I wouldn't have been surprised if he'd stayed at home. After all, Grandma had never approved of his marriage to my mother, let alone their subsequent separation and Dad's remarriage, and no longer being part of the family didn't disqualify one from being subject to her judgement, even from beyond the grave.

I loaded a plate from the buffet and retreated to the far end of the garden, where I could watch Tansy chase the local birds through the maze which had been installed during Grandma's first decade as Head Witch. I hadn't the faintest idea why she'd wanted a maze in the first place, but she'd built it on a piece of spare land that she and the Henbane Coven had been bickering over for decades in order to bring their argument to a halt. Hedges surrounded a fountain shaped like the head of a dragon, and a large oak tree sprawled near the back, effectively cutting off access from anywhere except the Wildwood Coven's back garden.

That stubborn Wildwood Witch trait had served her until the last, and her absence lingered among the sea of black cloaks and hats which dimmed the otherwise bright garden. I might have had ambivalent feelings towards my birth coven, but it'd take a while to adjust to not expecting to see my grandmother in the crowd in front of the whitewashed walls and arched windows of the coven's headquarters.

While I tried not to catch anyone's eye, a short witch with dark, curly hair detached herself from the crowd and perched next to me on the bench without asking for permission. It took me a moment to recognise her in her plain black cloak and hat, since the leader of the Henbane Coven usually wore bright clothing. *Speak of the devil... or witch, as it were.*

"Hello, Robin," said Tiffany Henbane. "I'm glad to see you came back for the funeral."

"Of course I did." Tiffany hadn't been a coven leader for very long herself, and I had little doubt some of her fellow Henbane witches would have hopes of snagging the position of Head Witch no matter how heavily the odds were stacked against them. "I was sorry to hear of her passing."

"As was I," she said. "It feels like she's always been around, doesn't it?"

I made a noncommittal noise, happy to be antisocial if it meant escaping an endless round of questions and comments from every stranger who'd noticed my return to town.

Unfortunately, not everyone picked up on my "leave me alone" vibes. Tiffany beckoned another witch over to join her, a redheaded teen dressed in robes which utterly swamped her. "This is Leona, my apprentice. Leona, this is Robin Wildwood."

Leona gave a shy smile. "Hi, Robin. I've heard all about you. Didn't you once set a swarm of birds loose in the classroom at the academy?"

Heat seared my neck, and I wondered how she knew about that years-old fiasco until I spotted the smile pulling at Tiffany's mouth. Had she been petty enough to tell her apprentice tales of my myriad failures? Apparently so.

"That's right." I refused to be goaded. "I did the same to a pair of nosy reporters who tried to corner me on my way into town and kept asking questions."

"Did you now?" Tiffany raised a delicately plucked brow. "I'm sure your mother has been careful to keep the press out. She's even sealed the gate at the back of the maze, did you know?"

"Uh huh." Since their own property was next door, I'd been willing to bet they'd spent the past few days snooping over the fence in the hopes of overhearing any gossip and had been bitterly disappointed to find the back gate sealed against them. "Can't be too careful."

"Of course not." She gave a tittering laugh. "Will your mother be keeping the maze, do you know?"

"Excuse me?" I blinked. "I imagine she will, yes."

Mum hadn't officially inherited the coven leader's headquarters yet, but I had little doubt she'd refuse to give up any gains her mother had made, especially if she found out the Henbane witches had tried to wrangle Grandma's maze back into her coven's hands at the former Head Witch's funeral. Tiffany had some nerve, that was for sure.

Before she could ask any more questions, however, a large tarantula crept across the lawn, and Leona gave a violent jump, dropping her plate. "I don't like spiders."

"I don't mind them so much." I sat back and watched their retreat, fighting a grin. When the crowd swallowed up both Tiffany and her apprentice, I crouched down to speak to the spider. "Where is she?"

The spider pointed a long leg at a gazebo nearby, where I spotted my cousin Rowan waving at me. I waved with one hand and picked up my plate with the other as I made my way over to her.

The spider, who happened to be called Ralph, crawled into the gazebo and climbed up his owner's shoulder. Rowan had freely admitted that the reason she'd chosen a tarantula as a familiar was due to her mother's fear of spiders, but she'd come to enjoy their company, and frankly, I could see the appeal of having an easy way to keep certain people at arm's length.

"Hey, Rowan." I ducked under the roof into the gazebo and sat on the bench inside. "Enjoy the funeral service?"

"Ugh," she said. "Whose idea was it to let Stacy ramble

on about Grandma for forty minutes? Frankly, I slept through the second half of it."

"Didn't your mother notice?" Perhaps not, given that she was under less scrutiny than I was, as the younger sibling who didn't expect to inherit the coven leadership even if her mother somehow managed to wrangle the job from mine.

"No, she was too busy glaring at *your* mother," she said. "They've been absolutely unbearable all week. Anyway, was that the Henbane Coven's leader?"

"Yeah, she wanted to know if the future coven leader was going to keep the maze."

"What a cheek." She pulled a face. "I expected their coven to take advantage of ours in a time like this, but not at Grandma's funeral."

"I know, right?" I shook my head. "At least the press weren't allowed in. I bet they're raging mad, but it serves them right."

The *Blue Moon* and similar local papers had been gossiping about Grandma's potential retirement for as long as I could remember, and it wouldn't have surprised me if she'd worked right up until her death at ninety-two purely to spite them.

"True," Rowan said. "So you're living in your old room again?"

"No, I didn't move back permanently," I said. "Why? Did someone tell you that?"

"Oh—no," she said. "I just assumed you wouldn't have come back if you had a choice."

"I couldn't skip out on the funeral, Rowan."

She dropped her gaze. "If I got away from here, it'd take more than a funeral to bring me back."

"You could, you know," I reminded her. "My mum would rather trade in her wand than admit the world outside of Wildwood Heath exists, but all you'd have to do is move outside the region, and nobody would recognise you."

My ability to talk to animals might have drawn attention in some circles, but delivering packages was a nondescript way to make a living. Rowan hadn't been old enough to move out on her own when I'd left town, but she'd turned twenty-one in the past year, and I assumed she had the same desire for freedom as I did.

She moved to the side of the gazebo to watch the garden without answering my comment. "I'm guessing they weren't grateful that you came back?"

"They expected *me* to be grateful they let me back into their house." I gave an eye roll. "At least they didn't ask me to give a speech at the funeral. They're too busy with their guests to bother with us."

"Famous last words." She took a step back. "We have company."

I peered past her, my heart sinking at the sight of the group approaching the gazebo. Mum and Ramsey walked alongside my cousin Vanessa and her mother, Aunt Shannon, as if they'd formed a united front to drag me away from my youngest cousin. Honestly. I knew Mum wasn't happy with me for keeping in touch with Rowan, but she wouldn't have got far by refusing to let me spend time with my one real friend among a sea of relatives with whom I had nothing in common.

Aunt Shannon and Vanessa looked more like twins despite the thirty-odd-year age gap between the two of them with the same perpetually sour expression and blond hair tied back underneath their pointed hats. Rowan, by contrast, had cut her darker blond hair into a pixie cut and would probably have dyed it bright pink if her mother hadn't put her foot down.

Aunt Shannon's gaze went to my feet. "What are you wearing?"

Oops. I'd pulled my cloak above my ankles, forgetting my inappropriately bright socks. "I didn't have time to do laundry before I flew here."

Aunt Shannon leaned closer to Mum. "I suppose each of us had to have at least one disappointing child, but I'm glad mine wasn't my first daughter. Rowan is fine with being the spare."

Anger rose within me, but Mum of all people interjected first. "I wouldn't make assumptions about what I think about my daughter. She's doing perfectly fine."

My mouth briefly fell open before I got my expression under control. Mum might be quick to criticise my own choices, but the one thing she wouldn't stand for was seeing other members of the coven belittle Ramsey and me. Even family. I shot Rowan a sympathetic look, but her gaze was on her feet, her shoulders drooping under her mother's withering stare. Another bolt of anger hit me, especially when Vanessa didn't come to her sister's defence.

Aunt Shannon had inherited the worst of the Wildwood family's competitive streak, and her scheming nature had led the local press to speculate that she'd had her ex-husband poisoned after he'd cheated on her. Despite the *Blue Moon*'s penchant for sensationalism, I for one wasn't quite sure it was *just* a rumour, since she was certainly ruthless when it came to getting what she wanted.

Aunt Shannon gave a false laugh. "I simply meant that it's a good idea to have a realistic idea of one's prospects. She's hardly Head Witch material, is she?"

"Technically, anyone can become Head Witch," I said. "Within the coven or otherwise."

"That's right," said Aunt Shannon. "There's no age limit on it either. An eleven-year-old child got the position in the northwest last year."

"Really?" I raised a brow. "Wow, that's got to be a blow to the egos of everyone who lost out."

Mum studied me. "Or an incentive to work harder."

Ouch. Just after she'd unexpectedly leapt to my defence, she'd made me wonder if part of her was lamenting the lost opportunity to have a prodigy for a daughter who'd landed the position of Head Witch before she'd hit puberty. Though I imagined if a minor ended up getting chosen, then an adult would make all the decisions for them anyway.

"Hard work has nothing to do with it," said Aunt Shannon. "The sceptre only chooses the worthy."

"If a kid can get chosen, then it doesn't say much for the rest of them," said Vanessa. "Maybe nobody else *was* worthy."

"That won't happen here," Mum said firmly. "We have a strong tradition of leadership in our family."

"Of course we do," said Aunt Shannon with a disparaging look at me. "We don't want anyone breaking that streak, do we? That's why this coven vote needs to focus on the future, not only the present."

I bristled like Prickles the hedgehog. Was she implying

that some of the witches on the council would vote against my mother tomorrow not because they didn't think she deserved the title but because they assumed that she'd eventually pass it onto her screwup of a daughter?

"Maybe the coven system is outdated," I said. "Coven leadership doesn't have to travel through the family line, let alone through the first daughter. Some other towns have more than one coven in charge, or they let the other paranormals have an equal say."

Aunt Shannon laughed. "What, the werewolves? They're animals who can barely get through a conversation without growling at one another."

I was willing to bet that was a pointed dig at my dad's new wife, which I didn't appreciate in the slightest. "Well, maybe if you'd left this town for once in your life, you'd think differently."

"Robin," Mum said in a warning tone.

Now everyone was staring at me. I knew my face was as red as Tansy's fur, but I refused to regret standing up for my dad and his family, who'd got so much hassle for their brief association with the coven that I was surprised he'd remained in Wildwood Heath afterwards.

A series of loud screeches above our heads broke the silence, and everyone's attention went to the sky as a flock of birds veered over the garden, drawn to the natural magic fizzling off my skin like static electricity.

"Robin." Mum's mouth moved so little that she'd rival a ventriloquist. "Calm down."

My hands curled into fists as I attempted to bring my magic under control before the birds brought an unfortunate storm upon the funeral guests. With a curl of her lip,

Aunt Shannon beckoned to her daughters. "We'll see which way the cards fall, won't we?"

As they left, I made a stealthy escape before Mum reprimanded me for rudeness that even she had to admit her sister had deserved. Ramsey always took her side, so it was no use appealing to him for backup, so I scanned for a way out. A few hundred funeral guests stood between me and the exit, but despite the security around the garden, I'd bet the secret passage out of the maze was still intact.

As I entered the maze, Tansy's head popped up from the nearest hedge. "You're running away."

"So are you."

"I wasn't on the guest list to begin with, remember?" she said. "Aren't you going to find Piper? I bet she'll be excited to see you."

"If she saw those birds, she'll know I'm here." I walked deeper into the maze, happy to let the sounds of the chattering witches and wizards fade into the background and the calmness of the forest wash over me. If I'd missed one thing while living in the city, it was this.

"You didn't use your magic, did you?" Tansy asked. "Honestly. Can't I take my eye off you for five seconds?"

"What were you even doing during the funeral?"

"Chasing pigeons."

"Right." I rubbed my forehead. "I never should have come back. It's just like before. Worse, even."

In the years since I'd turned eighteen, Mum had become louder and louder about her expectation that I'd be her successor as coven leader and possibly Head Witch —though the latter wasn't an inevitability even for a witch as powerful as her. Without Grandma, I hadn't a clue how they'd organise the ceremony in which the Head Witch's ceremonial sceptre would choose its next wielder. Everyone had grown used to the sceptre's magic settling on Grandma as its target, but the notion of letting an inanimate object decide the future of the coven struck me as absurd. They might as well swing the sceptre around like a game of spin the bottle and pick the person it landed on rather than expecting it to be consciously aware of who was worthy of the title. Generally, a coven leader took the title of Head Witch, perhaps because they'd already been voted into power by their peers, but gaining double the responsibility didn't strike me as much of a reward.

Regardless, Grandma had enjoyed the position, and Mum doubtlessly would too. But me? Not a chance. Aunt Shannon hadn't been wrong when she'd claimed I wasn't Head Witch material. Head Witches didn't accidentally unleash swarms of birds when they lost their tempers or misspell the word 'witch'.

Tansy, sensing my mood, jumped into my arms and wrapped her furry tail around my neck. "I could move those spiders you found in the wardrobe into your Aunt Shannon's room if you like."

I stifled a laugh. "You're welcome to try, as long as you don't get caught."

I glanced over the hedges, checking that I'd successfully shaken off anyone who might have followed me. Mum was too busy with the other guests to tail her wayward daughter, and Ramsey stuck to her like glue when they were at formal events. I didn't understand why he'd had to pick law enforcement over the coven, but Mum had given him a level of freedom she'd never afforded me.

Not that Mum would *directly* force me to stay. She'd simply keep needling me with reminders of everything I'd denied myself by leaving: a steady job, a roof over my head which wasn't subject to the whims of a landlord who couldn't be bothered to fix the broken heating system, and enough cash to buy the camera I wanted. Yet it was too much of a knock to my pride to throw myself on my family's mercy, and besides, I had more chance of winning the lottery than of following in her footsteps as Head Witch. Let's be realistic here.

Exhaling in a sigh, I made a mental note to message her when I got home, telling her I had a headache and that I was going to have an early night. For now, I rounded the corner and came to an abrupt halt in front of the fountain… and the body floating facedown in the water.

I remained completely still, as if suddenly approaching the body would make it stand up and walk away. Tansy jumped off me and approached the fountain, her tail standing on end. "Tell me she isn't dead."

"Okay, I won't tell you." I trod closer to the fountain, not recognising the red-haired witch who lay across the stone base, her hair swirling around the water. "Any idea who she is?"

Rustling sounded behind me, and Grandma's assistant, Stacy, ran into view. She stared at the fountain for a long moment, and then she screamed. Loudly.

The noise sent Tansy scurrying into retreat, and then the sound of footsteps thundered towards the maze. Several black-cloaked coven members appeared, erupting into exclamations when they saw the body in the fountain.

"That's Tessa," someone said. "Did she drown?"

"What's she doing in here?"

"Is that the Head Witch's granddaughter?"

"Out of the way." A clipped voice cut through the air, and the crowd parted to allow Mum to stride up to the fountain. Her gaze briefly travelled over to me before fixating on the body of the dead witch. "Who found her?"

"I did."

I'd figured she'd rather I admitted the truth, but the look on her face suggested otherwise. "I see."

More whispers travelled through the crowd, and Ramsey came hurrying in behind Mum. "All right, this is police business now. Everyone, get away from the fountain."

"Back into the garden," Mum ordered. "Nobody leave, is that clear?"

Everyone did as she asked without a word of dissent. Coven leader or not, they knew she was in charge here. Unfortunately, her manner suggested she blamed *me* for the ensuing chaos, as if I'd come into the maze expecting to find a dead body.

So much for a stealthy escape.

3

"Why," Tansy whispered, "do these things always seem to happen to you?"

"Very good question." I stood awkwardly with my back against the hedge as Ramsey drove the guests away from the crime scene, wondering when someone was going to fish poor Tessa out of the fountain. Of course, Mum was far more concerned with making sure nobody slipped away, and she guarded the maze's entrance while she barked out orders at everyone in the vicinity.

Aunt Shannon, naturally, had to intercede when Mum had a moment to breathe. "What does this mean for tomorrow's ceremony?"

"We'll deal with that later," Mum responded. "Once the police have made their assessment."

"Your son will understand the importance of the ceremony outweighs all other potential concerns, I'm sure."

"Well, someone did get murdered on the property," I

pointed out. "I doubt she fell into the fountain by accident."

"Robin, that's enough," Mum said without looking at me.

My hands curled into fists. I did not take kindly to being talked down to, especially as nobody had bothered to ask if I was okay. Stacy was in floods of tears nearby, but even in the face of disaster, I had to keep my composure and try not to look at poor Tessa's floating body. Part of me wondered if throwing up those delicious snacks from the buffet all over my shoes might give me an excuse to escape, but I did have a little dignity left. I swallowed hard and kept my gaze on the hedge instead, while Tansy climbed up to perch on my shoulder. "They'll have a hard job doing the ceremony without anyone to carry the sceptre."

"Oh, yeah." Tessa's job had been a simple one, but Mum would need to find a replacement before the ceremony. Besides, for all her authority, Mum wasn't coven leader yet, and some people wouldn't be thrilled if she decided to ignore the death of a young coven member in favour of pushing ahead with the ceremonies.

When the rest of the police showed up to help Ramsey remove the body from the fountain, I retreated towards the maze's entrance and found Stacy slumped on a bench nearby. She'd stopped crying, but she still looked shaken and pale when she lifted her head. "D-did you see T-Tessa go into the maze?"

I shook my head. "No. Did you?"

She slumped lower in her seat and shook her head. "I saw movement behind the hedges, but I didn't know she was in here."

"I wonder who pushed her in." I regretted my words when Stacy flinched so hard that she almost fell off the back of the bench, but nobody drowned in a shallow fountain by accident, and the timing set all my suspicions blaring.

Had someone killed Tessa in order to delay the coven leadership vote and the Head Witch ceremony? Mum had once pushed ahead with a coven meeting even when half its members had flu, though, and a dead body wouldn't stop her from putting a new coven leader in place.

As for Tessa herself, it wasn't as if she'd held a position anyone coveted. I was pretty sure carrying the ceremonial sceptre would have been her first major event as a coven member, though it was beyond me to figure out what she'd even been doing in the maze. Maybe she'd been trying to escape the crowd like I had.

Stacy tremulously got to her feet and walked away, past Tiffany Henbane and her apprentice, Leona. Their group stood in a huddle, perhaps discussing how Tessa's death had put a wrench in her schemes to get her hands on the maze. Aunt Shannon's sharp voice brought Stacy to a startled halt. I didn't hear what she said, but Stacy backed up, trembling, while I suppressed the urge to tell her to leave the poor girl alone. She might have droned on too much during the funeral, but she'd had as traumatic an experience as I had and was now jobless for the foreseeable future unless the next coven leader opted to hire her as their assistant, which was by no means a guarantee. She did most of the work for the coven that nobody else wanted to, since Grandma's ancient cat familiar spent most of his time sleeping, but the new coven leader might be more hands-on. Mum certainly was.

Vanessa chimed in with her mother, while Stacy hurried back towards the maze with her head down. Rowan wasn't with them, perhaps having taken the chance to sneak off home while everyone was distracted. I didn't blame her a bit, but I couldn't help thinking back to Aunt Shannon's insinuations about my side of the family's fitness to run the coven. When our gazes locked across the garden, I gave her a flat stare. I'd bet she was all too keen to blame me for ruining the week's plans by finding a dead body, but I suspected I'd have to take the brunt of the reprimands from my immediate family.

As if conjured by my thoughts, Ramsey emerged from the maze and made a beeline for me. "I wish you hadn't been the one to find the body," he said in an undertone. "Why were you sneaking around the maze in the first place?"

"I needed some air."

He raised a brow. "You were already outside."

I rolled my eyes at him. "There was hardly room to breathe in the garden. I swear half the guests weren't even local. What will you do if one of *them* turns out to have bumped off Tessa?"

He shot me a disapproving look. "Now isn't the time to jump to conclusions."

"She can't have drowned herself, Ramsey." I kept my voice low. "This was murder, and in the coven's garden at that."

"I doubt it was an accident," he said begrudgingly, "but it's more than likely someone she was close to was responsible, not a guest from the other side of the country. That said, since you were the one who found her body, I have to question you first."

"You've got to be joking." He must have been. Right? "Mum doesn't think I'd throw someone into a fountain to get out of a family event, does she?"

Ramsey's lips pressed together. "Look, I can strike you off the list if there's nothing you haven't told me."

"You think I'm lying." Disbelief flooded my voice. "I walked into the maze and saw Tessa's body in the fountain. Tansy spotted her first, if you want to nitpick, but I'm telling the truth."

"I believe you," he said, "but if anything implicating our family gets out, the press will have a field day."

I muttered a few words which made him give me another look of disapproval. "The press is not allowed in. If they spin some nonsense story out of this, they have zero evidence to back it up. Anyway, do you think someone who wants the coven leadership might be responsible?"

His expression flattened. "Don't you even think about saying that in front of Mum."

"But do you think so?" I pressed. "Who else is on the suspect list?"

"Not you," he said. "You should head back to the house before Mum decides to keep you under her watch while I question all the other guests."

Funnily enough, his order made me want to do the opposite. If someone wanted to disrupt the choosing of the next Head Witch, what was to stop them from going after my family next? Mum and Ramsey might annoy me on a regular basis, but I refused to entertain the possibility of them being targeted by a murderer.

On the other hand, every single member of the town's law enforcement was inside this very garden, so there was nowhere safer. If anything, it made me uneasy about walking back to the coven's headquarters alone.

As I stepped onto the paved area, a shadow fell over me from behind. I halted and spun on my heel, while a man took a step back, hands raised. "Whoa. Didn't mean to startle you. I just didn't think you should be walking around alone at night."

He looked vaguely familiar, though I couldn't figure out where I'd seen him before. Tall, dark hair, broad shoulders... and an appealing smile which crossed his mouth when we locked eyes. Hang on. "Harvey?"

"That's me," he said. "I didn't get the chance to say hi earlier, but I was at school with you, remember?"

"Of course I remember you," I said.

He'd changed a lot, though not enough for me to forget that I *might* have had a slight crush on him when we'd been at the local academy. Unrequited, mind. We'd moved in different circles, since he was the athletic type who'd been flying on a broomstick since he could walk and had competed in the region's youth Sky Hopper League. After we'd left school, I hadn't thought I'd ever see him again, much less as a tall and very attractive adult.

"Good," he said. "Are you heading home?"

"Yeah," I said. "Ramsey's going to be here for a while. So is my mum."

"I figured." He glanced over his shoulder. "I can't believe what happened to that girl. Did they say someone murdered her?"

Already? Maybe Ramsey had a point about the speed at which rumours generated themselves and spread through our small community. "Nobody's saying anything for certain so far. You were at the funeral, then?"

"Yeah." He fell into step with me as we made our way through the dark entryway of the witches' headquarters and out the front door onto the equally dark road. "I was in the back row, since I'm not part of the Wildwood Coven. I'm sorry for your loss."

"Grandma and I weren't close to one another," I replied.

"Right, I remember that too."

Did he? In fairness, being related to the Head Witch was a natural source of attention, and it hadn't exactly been a secret that I'd been the black sheep of the family. Or red squirrel, as the case may be. While he wasn't part of the coven, everyone in town had grown used to Grandma being the Head Witch, since she'd held the title before I was born and had been leader of the Wildwood Coven even longer. This was the end of an era in more than one sense.

"What do you do now?" I asked, in an attempt to change the subject. "For a living, I mean?"

"I'm the captain of the regional Sky Hopper team," he said. "I also coach at the academy in my free time."

"Oh, nice." I vaguely remembered him saying way back when we'd been kids that he wanted to play Sky Hopper professionally, and while his family hadn't expected him to be able to make a career of it, it sounded like they'd at least let him try. I had to admit it made me smile a little to know at least one of us had achieved their dreams. It also made me feel vaguely guilty for squandering the chances I'd been given, even if it had been no fault whatsoever of my own.

"What about you?" he asked. "Are you moving back here, then?"

"No—definitely not." Did he look disappointed? It must have been a trick of the light. "I already have a job as a courier. I travel all over."

"Oh, that sounds fun," he said. "The best part of playing sports is getting to see interesting places. Though I suppose the coven leader does get to do the same. And the Head Witch."

"Yeah, they do." I gave a wry smile. "They sometimes get to move from one meeting room to another."

That made him laugh. "You never know. Things might change when the new leader takes over."

"Maybe." It wasn't as if I'd been around here much myself for the last few years, but I knew better than to think I could get Mum to part ways with the coven's myriad traditions. It would be like trying to convince Tansy not to chase the local birds.

Harvey came to a halt when we reached the right house. "Here we are. I hope we run into each other again before you leave."

"Same." I shot him a smile before entering the house in a better mood despite my lingering worries over Tessa's fate and what that meant for the rest of us. Running into him had been a pleasant surprise and a nice distraction from what had otherwise been a terrible day in every capacity. Not that I'd come here expecting a good time, but still.

As I entered the hall, Tansy scurried through the open door behind me. "You're not going to drop this one, are you?" she whispered in my ear. "Finding the murderer, I mean."

"It looks like I'm here for the duration now anyway," I

muttered. "I mean, if someone wants to sabotage the choosing of the next coven leader or Head Witch, then drowning someone on the property is one way to go about it."

Did the murderer want to delay the coven leadership ceremony? Or was the title of Head Witch their target? I closed the door behind me and walked through the darkened hallway, startling when a pair of claws grabbed my ankle and a yowl hit my eardrums.

"Ow!" I hopped on one leg, yelping, and scrambled for the light switch. Tansy found it first, and the hall lights illuminated the half-bald, half-fluffy dark shape of Grandma's familiar. "Don't scare me like that, Carmilla."

I hadn't set eyes on Carmilla since I'd returned home, and to be honest, I'd forgotten Grandma's familiar was still around. She'd once spent every waking moment at her owner's side, but in recent years, she'd spent most of her time sleeping in her room instead.

"Meow." The little black cat put on a reproachful tone.

"Meow?" I echoed. "Have you forgotten how to talk?"

"Didn't you hear?" Tansy said. "She hasn't said a word to anyone else in the family since her witch died."

"No, I didn't hear." I crouched down to give the cat a stroke, only for her to generously apply her claws to my hand the same way she'd done to my ankle. "Ow!"

"Meow." She stalked away and curled up on the carpet further down the hallway, no doubt to attempt to trip my brother up when he eventually returned home.

"Poor kitty." I shook my painful hand, wondering just how many other surprises the week would throw at me. It shouldn't have surprised me that the universe would throw murder into the mix, but if I wanted to get anywhere, I needed to actually convince Mum that it *was* murder.

4

I awoke late the following morning, disorientated after a restless night of bad dreams of being chased through the maze by an unseen figure. I blinked at the stripes of light illuminating the shapes of the old furniture in my childhood bedroom before going to the window to check on my familiar. I assumed Tansy had gone outside to chase the local birds around, and sure enough, when I looked outside, I spotted a bright-red tail waving from the fence as Tansy executed an impressive flying leap onto the bird feeder. At least one of us was having a good time.

Yawning, I went to the wardrobe and found it packed with Mum's spare cloaks. Mum had a walk-in closet in her own room, so it was anyone's guess as to why she needed to use my wardrobe as well. Mercifully, I wasn't expected to dress respectfully for a funeral today, so I put on my jeans and my *Lord of the Rings* hoody before heading downstairs.

Someone—presumably Mum—had turned the carpets in the hall and on the stairs jet black, along with the wallpaper. I could only assume that she'd intended it to last within the period of mourning for the former Head Witch and that they'd go back to normal at the end of the week, because the gloominess made the place resemble a haunted house. At least they hadn't done the same to my room, because the black-draped furniture in the living room looked like something out of a low-budget performance of *Dracula,* especially with Carmilla sleeping on the sofa. Her silence was slightly ominous after our encounter last night, so I opted against waking her up to stroke her.

Mum and Ramsey sat at the kitchen table, both of them eating cereal. Given the circles under Mum's eyes, it was possible she hadn't actually gone to bed, and Ramsey looked like he wouldn't mind joining Horace, who'd curled up to sleep on another chair. Luckily for all of us, I spotted him before I sat down and got myself clawed again.

Dishes were stacked on the side, a sign that the cleaner hadn't been around. Neither had the cook, because instead of a cooked breakfast, there didn't seem to be anything on offer but cold cereal. I was starving enough not to care, so I poured myself a sizeable bowlful and tried to figure out the fancy coffee maker.

"Are the staff not in?" I asked.

"I gave them the week off," Mum said in crisp tones. "We have too unpredictable a schedule until after the new Head Witch is chosen."

My mouth parted. It struck me as a strange choice, but maybe Mum wanted privacy to go through Grandma's things without the cleaning staff around. Or the gardener, which would explain why she'd been trimming the roses herself yesterday. "What's the deal with Carmilla? Has she really not said a word since Grandma passed away?"

"No," said Prickles, who sat on the table with a saucer of milk in front of him. "She had a nasty shock."

"She got her claws in me and tried to trip me up when I walked into the house last night."

"Speaking of which," said Ramsey, "who on earth did you go home with? I saw you walking into the coven's headquarters with a strange man."

Ah. "Harvey offered to walk me home. We went to school together."

"Who?" he asked. "Is he with the coven?"

"No, he isn't, and you must know who he is. He's captain of the local Sky Hopper team."

"Is he?" Mum's hands clenched around her coffee mug. "You went off alone with a stranger?"

"He's not a stranger," I said. "He's not part of any coven, so there's zero chance of him being in the running either for the coven leader title or for Head Witch, which doesn't give him any reason to have murdered Tessa. And yes, I still think she was murdered."

"Her death was officially declared a homicide," Ramsey said slowly, as if the words pained him to say. "And on that note, I need to check into the office. Can you please try to stay out of trouble?"

"Only if you try to educate yourself on the local sports teams." I gave him an eye roll. "Prickles, don't tell me he hasn't been supporting our prizewinning team? I'm shocked."

The hedgehog hopped off the table to join his owner. "Your brother is more concerned with the safety of the coven than with frivolous games."

"Or with having a life." I probably shouldn't have said that, but his and Mum's comments about Harvey had rubbed me up the wrong way. Would they rather I'd walked home alone with a potential killer on the loose?

Ramsey went pink and left the kitchen without another word. Mum, meanwhile, rose to her feet and went to the sink to wash the dishes. I could count on one hand the number of times I'd seen her do any chores. Why *had* she dismissed the staff for the week? This went beyond her dislike of anyone being in the house when she wasn't here. No… there was something more going on.

I finished my cereal and approached the sink with my bowl in hand. "If Tessa's death was a homicide, are we potential targets for the killer?"

Mum's shoulders tensed. "Not officially, and don't say a word of the sort to anyone else. We've already had to delay the vote on the next coven leader until your brother has finished questioning all the council members about Tessa's death."

My brows shot up. "The council members were all named as suspects? Bet they loved that."

"Everyone in the coven is a suspect," she said. "And so is everyone outside of the coven who was present at the funeral."

"And what if someone from outside town sneaked in through the maze?"

"They can't have," said Mum. "I put a ward on the place to stop those wretched reporters getting in, and that giant tree at the back took care of the rest."

That still left a lot of potential murderers, and the idea of waiting for my brother to question every single person who had been at the funeral was about as appealing as riding a splinter-laden broomstick. "I should check on my familiar."

"Where are you going?" She gave me a hard stare as I made for the front door. "You can't go wandering around alone."

"It's broad daylight, Mother," I pointed out. "Besides, what am I supposed to do, sit in the house and twiddle my thumbs?"

I couldn't even get a decent internet signal in the house at the best of times, and I hadn't brought much with me except for a small suitcase and a broomstick.

"There's plenty to do to help prepare for the ceremonies."

I'd walked right into that one. "You said yourself that everything was on hold until the questioning is over. Look, I'll be fine."

As I closed the front door behind me, I reached into my bag for a packet of nuts—Tansy's favourites. I hadn't even opened the packet before she came scurrying along the fence from the back garden to nab a tasty treat from my hand. "Where are you off to?"

"Anywhere I might avoid coven drama." I headed past Aunt Shannon's house and made for one of the nature trails in the woods. One of the upsides to growing up in Wildwood Heath was that there was no shortage of woodland to explore, and I'd much preferred roaming the nature trails to staying confined to the garden, where Mum kicked up a fuss if I touched any of her prizewin-ning flowers or left muddy footprints on the paving stones.

Tansy occupied herself chasing birds out of the nearby trees while I walked on a meandering route through the woods, the hum of magic in the background a reminder of another upside to being home. My coven's magic was stronger the closer we stood to the Wildwood, and for most of us, accessing it in the woods was like drawing water out of a natural spring. Mine, on the other hand, behaved more like a geyser, which meant being at home made it even more liable to explode out of my control when I lost my temper. I'd never quite managed to convince certain members of my family that it wasn't intentional.

While I'd always felt safe amid the thick trees and the sound of birdsong, Mum's obvious concern that I might get jumped had rattled me more than I wanted to let on. If the killer wanted to get at the coven leadership position, I wasn't exactly the first person they'd target, but why had they gone after Tessa to begin with? Strange and unnerving. I found myself tensing at small noises in the bushes despite the buzz of my coven magic telling me they were only birds or small rodents. Logically, I was more likely to get ambushed by more reporters than a murderer, which wasn't much of a reassuring thought.

I looped around the path to retrace my steps home, where I heard two familiar voices drifting from the direction of the house.

"What do you mean, she went out?" asked a male voice. "Did you send her to run errands for the coven?"

"Of course I didn't," Mum retaliated. "By all means, go and look for her yourself. You know the woods well enough, don't you?"

I waited for the sound of the door closing behind her before approaching the short, round wizard from behind. "Hey, Dad."

"How's my favourite daughter?" He turned around with a grin and wrapped me in a bear hug. "I wanted to meet you after the funeral, but I heard there was an incident of some kind."

"Yeah… a girl drowned in the fountain." I was glad he'd missed being caught up in that. "Tessa. She worked for the coven."

"Someone died?" His eyes widened. "I did wonder if there was a reason it was so quiet in town."

"Yeah, everyone who was at the funeral is being questioned." By my brother, but it couldn't be clearer that he'd neglected to tell Dad any of the details. To be honest, I didn't think Ramsey had ever quite forgiven him for leaving when we were kids, though even back then, I'd understood that our dad hadn't abandoned us intentionally. When Mum was wronged, she didn't forgive *or* forget, so when she'd kicked him out of the house, it'd been pretty much final.

Mum claimed she didn't care that he'd met and married a werewolf since then, but given the attitudes of people like Aunt Shannon, I could understand why she wouldn't bring up her ex that often. As for poor Dad, I felt bad for not going to visit him sooner.

He nodded, the corners of his mouth turning down. "Hell of a homecoming, right?"

"Tell me about it," I said. "I just went for a walk to get away from it all. How's Jessica?"

"She's great," he said. "The kids are too. Real bundles of

energy. She's taking them to school, while I have a job in about… five minutes. I should run."

"You're still doing repairs?"

"You bet," he said. "Might not be glamorous, but the work never goes away as long as these wizards keep doing a shoddy job with their construction spells."

"Hey, I'm a courier for rich wizards, so I can't say anything about lack of glamour," I said. "I booked the week off to come here, and I'm starting to have regrets."

"I don't blame you, but I'm glad I was able to drop by and see you," he said. "You're here all week?"

"With luck, that'll be all," I said. "I'll try to drop by the house sometime when you aren't too busy."

He beamed. "Anytime. Jess and the kids will be glad to see you."

That makes one person, at least. While doing odd repair jobs didn't pay particularly well, Dad was happy enough, and despite what certain members of my family might say, it was a perfectly respectable way of making a living.

While he departed, my gaze lingered on the front door to the house for a moment. If Mum was waiting to berate me about my dad, then she'd have to wait a little longer, because if it was true that hardly anyone was outside, there was no better time for me to see if the rest of Wildwood Heath had changed in the past few years.

The town's main road was more of a meandering trail between rows of small shops and cafés owned and run by the town's residents, since paranormal rural communities didn't typically do chains. A few new shops had popped up, but the old staples were still in place, including the werewolf-run café called Were's My Coffee? Everyone groaned at the name, but their lattes were as good as any witch-made ones, if not better.

I ducked inside the café, perusing the updated menu and relishing the ordinariness of the chatter in the background as I paid for my latte. I blew on it to cool it down before taking a sip that brought a rush of nostalgia. Pity I couldn't keep the upsides of Wildwood Heath and ditch the downsides.

A hand snagged my arm on the way out, nearly causing me to drop that delicious coffee. My heart sank as I found myself nose to nose with Clarice and Speck, the former still wielding her microphone like a weapon. "Robin! We didn't get an interview with you yesterday, but you must have some words to say on the Head Witch's funeral and why everyone left in such a secretive manner."

I had a few choice words I'd have liked to say which wouldn't be repeatable on live TV, but I knew Mum would tell me to hold my tongue and not give them any ammunition. What they thought had gone down at the funeral was a mystery I had zero interest in knowing the answer to, though I should have guessed they'd stayed in town overnight despite not being allowed to attend. Mum had been clear that none of them were to enter the house or set foot within ten feet of our property throughout the entire week. She knew what lengths they'd go to in order to get a good story.

"Sorry, I can't stick around and chat," I said in as pleasant a tone as I could muster. "I have somewhere to go."

Namely, as far away as possible.

"Of course you do," said Clarice. "If you'd like to do an exclusive interview with us, then here's my card."

"Right." Unenthusiastically, I took the card without looking at her and walked out the door... straight into someone coming the other way. My latte fell from my hand, drenching both me and Harvey. Luckily, more of it went on me than on him, but of all the people to walk into, it just had to be him.

"I'm so sorry!" I exclaimed. "I should have looked where I was going."

"Don't worry about it." He reached for a nearby table and picked up a heap of napkins, while I set about hastily dabbing at my soaked hoody. The flash of a camera made me swivel around and give Clarice and Speck a death glare. I wished I'd spilled the coffee on their fancy recording equipment instead.

"Wait," I protested when Harvey made for the counter to get me a replacement latte. When Clarice and Speck made another attempt to get close to me, I turned my back and wiped the coffee off my face until Harvey returned.

"Come on." Latte in hand, Harvey held the door open for me so that I didn't walk into him this time. "Better get away from them."

"I guess I should be thankful to the murderer," I said, taking the paper cup from him, "considering that in any other week, my coffee-soaked face would be on the front page."

Harvey's expression turned mildly alarmed, while I wished I could stuff the words back into my mouth. "Should I report them for hassling you?"

"To whom?" I asked. "The entire police department is tied up with the murder investigation. Besides, even my mother has trouble stopping the press from ramming their noses into our business. They're not technically breaking the law."

The most she'd managed to do was ban them from the coven's territory, but that hadn't stopped them from waiting for the first opportunity to pounce on anyone who ventured outside.

"That's ridiculous." He fell into step with me as I walked back through the town. "I wondered if I'd run into you again before you left, but I didn't expect it to be that literal."

"Ha." I slowed my pace when we'd left the café in the dust, holding the latte with both hands to prevent any further mishaps. "Well, I'm stuck here until after the new coven leader and Head Witch are confirmed. And until my brother finishes the questioning."

"So he definitely thinks it's murder, then?" he asked. "No, wait… never mind. I shouldn't pry."

"Don't worry about it," I said. "I'm pretty sure it's the entire town's business at this point. Besides, murder isn't something you can sweep under the carpet."

Maybe it was the fact that my brother had refused to listen to me and that Mum wasn't even acknowledging me at the moment, but I didn't mind him asking questions. If anything, I welcomed the chance to talk with an objective outsider who didn't have any stake in the coven's leadership whatsoever.

"Did you know the girl who died?" he asked.

"Not well," I said, "but she worked for the coven and was meant to be involved in the ceremony where the new Head Witch will be chosen. Not great timing."

"Your brother is head of the law enforcement, right?" he said. "He'll get to the bottom of it, I'm sure."

"Yeah." I put on a false smile as we reached the end of my road. "I should head home and change. Thanks for the coffee."

"Anytime." He left while I walked on, sipping slowly at my latte to ensure I didn't spill another drop. At least I'd wrecked Clarice and Speck's business card as well as drenching my clothes, but if I *did* show up on the front page of the papers, I'd have to think of a worse revenge scheme than setting a bunch of birds on them.

Would Mum want to know the press were still hounding me? It wasn't as if I'd said anything which alluded to yesterday's events, but she was in a tetchy mood already. Everyone in the coven would remain tense and sleep deprived until the coven leader and Head Witch were confirmed and they could go back to some semblance of normality. The press would have to stay away from the ceremony, at least.

Tansy ran into view across the front lawn as I approached the house. "Where have you been?"

"Went to get a coffee." I drank the rest of my latte and crumpled the cup in my hand.

"Looks like you took a swim in it."

"The press tried to ambush me." I unlocked the door, resigning myself to another unwelcome conversation with Mum on my way to change out of my soaked jeans and hoody.

Instead, I found Aunt Shannon reclining on the living room sofa as though she lived here. Both cats stood in the doorway, hissing at her, but neither of them had managed to herd her outside. The giant magpie sitting on her knee might have been part of the reason, as well as the wand sticking out of her pocket.

"There you are, Robin," she said. "Your mother isn't around, so I let myself in. I hope you don't mind."

Yes, I do mind. "Where's Mum, then?"

"Haven't a clue." Her tone was entirely too cheerful. "So I thought I'd have a chat with you about that girl's murder."

5

I stared at my aunt for an instant. "Ramsey is the one doing the questioning, remember?"

Why on earth had she invited herself into Mum's house? In the absence of the usual household staff, I assumed I was supposed to offer her a cup of tea or something, but I didn't particularly want to take my eyes off Myrtle the magpie in case she started a fight with the cats or with Tansy.

My aunt solved my dilemma by walking into the kitchen herself while I washed the coffee stains off my hands and hoped I'd at least got most of it off my face.

"You're jumpy," Aunt Shannon observed.

I can't imagine why. "I found a dead body yesterday, remember? Speaking of which, did you already talk to my brother?"

"You mean to ask if I suffered through him asking me questions?" She sniffed. "Imagine doing that to your own family."

"We're not immune to the law, Aunt Shannon."

"Pity, that," she said.

I dearly hoped she didn't mean to imply we *should* be allowed to get away with murder. "Did you know Tessa at all?"

"Why do you ask?"

I shrugged in an attempt at casualness. "I don't know anything about her, and you wanted to discuss the murder. Tessa wasn't that high up in the coven. She didn't even get a vote on the council, did she?"

"That doesn't mean her word held no sway over the others."

What did that mean? That someone had been intending to harm the coven by killing her? "I have no idea what you're talking about. You think the killer might have their eyes on other people in the coven too?"

"Is that what you believe?"

Her direct question was disconcerting, to say the least, and I hadn't the faintest clue what she'd expected me to say in response. "I believe this is a mess, frankly."

The door opened, and Mum walked into the house from the garden. I'd been beginning to wonder where she'd disappeared to. "Shannon, what are you doing here?"

"Your daughter and I are discussing yesterday's tragedy," she said. "And whether the killer is likely to strike again before the main event."

"Are you, now?" Mum put on a withering look. "I hardly think they would dare. As for the ceremony, it will go ahead tomorrow as planned, after the council have voted in their new leader."

Will it? "And… the Head Witch ceremony?"

"That will be held at the same time."

"Really?" Aunt Shannon raised a brow. "That seems rather bold. If the person who's chosen as Head Witch isn't the same as the individual who becomes coven leader, then you run the risk of undermining the coven leader's authority. We need stability in these trying times."

I blinked at her. "You think someone who isn't from the coven might end up claiming the sceptre?"

"Certainly *not,*" Mum said. "Shannon, don't be absurd. You know perfectly well nobody outside of the coven is remotely qualified for the position."

What was Aunt Shannon playing at? Perhaps she was trying to get a rise out of Mum intentionally. After all, if an outsider got the position, she'd lose out too. Twice over, if Mum ended up taking the position of coven leader.

Which she would. She had to.

A smile played on Aunt Shannon's mouth, while Mum's glare made me want to creep out of the room before wands came out and sparks started flying. I didn't *think* they'd start duelling, but emotions had been running high from the get-go, and now their wishes for a straightforward coven leadership ceremony had been thoroughly trounced.

"If you're certain," said Aunt Shannon. "I assume you've chosen a temporary replacement for Tessa."

"Yes," said Mum. "Robin will be taking on her role."

My heart skipped a beat. "Excuse me?"

"Tessa is dead, and we haven't the time to hire a replacement," she said. "You've been to enough ceremonies that you ought to be familiar with how things are meant to work."

I stared at her in disbelief. "Not in a coven leadership ceremony. Or a Head Witch one, come to that."

"Exactly." Aunt Shannon looked me up and down. "Look at the state of her. She even has coffee stains on her clothes."

"I was on my way to change when I found you'd let yourself into the house," I said through gritted teeth. "My mother and I are going to talk about this. Alone."

Aunt Shannon sidled towards the kitchen door, her gaze roving over Mum with an expression of mingled anger and defiance. Mum watched her go, her eyes narrowed, while Aunt Shannon's magpie familiar flew after her in a sweep of wings.

I followed Mum into the hallway, seeing both cats dart into the living room upon Aunt Shannon's departure and settle down on the sofa.

Mum firmly closed the front door. "Would you rather I gave the job to Vanessa?"

No. But I hardly needed another reason to stick around… or become a target. It was bad enough the entire coven being around to witness if I managed to screw up again. "Vanessa has more experience than I do."

Instead of answering, Mum strode into the living room and retrieved a pile of robes from an armchair. "Go upstairs and try these on. You'll wear them for the ceremony, and I need to see if they have to be adjusted to your size."

I didn't take them. "Are we going to talk compensation? Because if I'm going to be volunteered for Tessa's job, I'll need a better reason to paint a target on my head."

"You aren't a target," she said. "As for compensation, I'll see about that camera of yours."

If I'd been holding anything, I might have dropped it. "Excuse me?"

"You wanted it, didn't you?"

I wanted to pay for it with my own hard-earned cash. I bit the inside of my cheek. "Yes, but it's pricey."

"Money doesn't matter." She waved a hand. "Go on, get changed."

I stood in a daze, caught between the impulse to take what I could get and the urge to lean into my withering sense of pride and refuse. She must really need my help if she was willing to grant me my wish, but why had she discarded the possibility of me being targeted by the killer so readily?

"Mum, do you know what Tessa—"

She retreated from the room. "I have an hour to spare. If you don't have those robes on in five minutes, I'll give the job to Vanessa."

"She has got to be joking," I murmured to Carmilla, who simply meowed at me from the sofa.

Next to her, Horace lifted his head. "She isn't. And she means what she says."

"Vanessa *does* have more experience than I do." On the other hand, Rowan would be crushed if she found out I'd given her sister the chance to show off in front of the coven, and the last thing I wanted to do was to give Aunt Shannon more reasons to belittle me.

Besides, Tessa's only job had been to carry the ceremonial sceptre to the centre of the hall and wait for it to pick a new wielder. Grandma's *cat* had once held that job, and I could just see Aunt Shannon telling the entire coven that an ancient feline was more competent than the former Head Witch's granddaughter.

Mind made up, I went upstairs to change before resigning myself to spending the next hour being poked and prodded as Mum adjusted the robes to the right size. It took a great deal of self-control not to bombard her with questions, but starting an argument with my mum while she was wielding pointy objects wasn't likely to end well.

I regretted my silence when she started dropping hints that I needed to bring Tansy in to help her learn how to help me out when I was coven leader myself. Even the promise of the new camera felt less like compensation and more like bribery to lead up to the inevitable moment when she asked me to stay in Wildwood Heath forever.

Ramsey came into the living room while Mum was off hunting for more needles. "Is that a new cloak?"

"Supposedly, I can't do the ceremony wearing just any old cloak." I winced as a needle snagged my bare wrist when I moved my arm. "I'm Tessa's replacement. Temporarily."

He didn't look remotely surprised. "Good. That'll make things easier."

"I didn't know I needed to stand for an hour being measured for a two-minute ceremonial role," I added. "Be glad you only have to interrogate potential murderers. Learned anything?"

"No," he said. "Except that an awful lot of people seem to have a guilty conscience. If I was to accuse any of them based on the elaborate excuses they concocted for whatever they were doing when Tessa was killed, I'd have to arrest half the town."

"But you haven't made any actual arrests yet?" I asked. "Have you gone through the whole coven?"

"No, just the senior members and anyone who was close to the victim," he said. "As of yet, no arrests, but I didn't expect the killer to confess outright."

"That'd be too easy." I rolled my shoulders, which ached from standing with my arms outstretched for so long. "What do you think, then? Personal grudge or a reason to worry for the rest of us?"

"The only thing that concerns me is that half the council is blaming their grievances about the coven leadership ceremony being delayed on me."

"That's because everyone's too scared to blame Mum."

People respected my brother, but they weren't outright terrified of him the way they were of Mum and the way they'd been of Grandma.

"Everyone's worried and stressed, which makes it hard to tell if they're lying," he said. "It's possible Tessa had an argument with someone which nobody has mentioned yet, but so far, all we can work out is that she didn't speak to anyone after the funeral and went straight into the maze."

"And someone ambushed her," I concluded. "I didn't see anyone go into the maze while I was sitting outside, but I can't say I was paying full attention."

The first person who'd come to talk to me had been Tiffany of the Henbane Coven, before Rowan had come to my rescue and then Aunt Shannon and the others had interrupted us. If I'd gone into the maze before I'd met Rowan, might I have run into the killer? Or caught them in the act? It was impossible to say.

"Oh, yeah. I saw Dad earlier."

"Did you?" His tone was carefully neutral.

"Have you talked to him recently?"

"No," he said. "We live in the same town, though. It's not like I left for years like you did."

"Ouch." I pressed a hand to my chest. "I'm wounded. Besides, I'm sure Dad would like to hear from you."

He made a noncommittal grunt. "He can tell me himself."

I opened my mouth to tell him it wasn't Dad's fault that he hadn't been able to say a proper goodbye to either of us after Mum had kicked him out right after he'd asked for a divorce, but he was already walking away, presumably to find Mum and give her the same update he'd given me. Pressuring him on Dad was probably a futile task this week considering the stress he must be under. While this might not be his first murder case, I doubted he'd ever questioned the most prominent members of his own coven beforehand.

A grunt of surprise came from the hallway, followed by a yowl from Carmilla. Ramsey, who'd presumably come close to treading on her on his way upstairs, hopped out of reach of her claws.

"She was lying right in the way," he protested. "I didn't see her."

"She did that to me when I came back from the funeral." I studied the half-bald black cat, who looked reproachfully back at me. "Hey, Carmilla. Remembered how to speak yet?"

"She's grieving," Ramsey said, rubbing his ankle. "Give her time."

I studied the cat's squashed face, and a sudden suspicion hit me like a lightning bolt. Grandma had been fine up until the moment she'd died, by all accounts, and her death had been sudden enough to take even Mum by surprise. Yeah, she'd been *old,* but how many scheming individuals had been waiting to take advantage of her retirement? Did Carmilla suspect her witch hadn't died of natural causes? Was that why she'd stopped talking to all of us?

Mum descended the stairs, her loud footsteps interrupting my whirling thoughts. "Oh, there you are, Ramsey. Did you find anything out from the people you questioned?"

"Unfortunately not." He stepped aside to allow her to pass by, while Carmilla slunk away, presumably to lie in another hazardous spot. "None of the higher coven members have demonstrated any motive to murder Tessa."

"As I expected." Mum herded us into the living room, where she proceeded to start sticking pins in my robe again.

I squirmed under Mum's sharp grip as she rearranged the pins in my sleeve. "So the investigation is over?"

"No," he said. "I'm going to talk to a few other people who were present at the funeral and then piece together what I have so far, but I don't expect to have a verdict by the day's end."

"I see." Mum's tone was neutral, almost bored. "That will make things easier for the process of the ceremony tomorrow."

"Is Tessa's funeral going to be before or after the ceremony?" I asked.

"After," she said curtly. "That'll be up to her family, but the longer we delay the vote for the next coven leader, the more likely it is that we'll run into opposition."

"From whom?"

Aunt Shannon? The press had speculated for years about her murdering her ex-husband, though he'd been an unpleasant man, and nobody had been sorry when he'd died of a heart attack not long after he'd been found out to be cheating on his wife. It was way too early for me to jump to conclusions, but she was one of the most scheming people I knew. Enough to kill her own mother, though? Surely not. Besides, I should have known better than to believe the press, given that they'd once run a double-page spread speculating that Grandma had only lived so long because she drank the blood of her predecessors, vampire style. I didn't even know where to start with that one.

"Anyone who disagrees with the way my mother ran things," Mum said. "And anyone who wishes to intervene before the coven has a strong new leadership in place."

She was pretty much running the coven already, and everyone seemed happy enough to let her do just that. What was she so worried about? If Tessa had been murdered by someone with a personal grudge, then she wouldn't have had the same impetus to start cancelling events and acting as though there was an axe murderer stalking us. She certainly wouldn't have warned me off walking in the woods. No, she suspected more was at play, and if we shared the same suspicion, at least she wouldn't be alone. Even if not, then it was worth the temporary short-term conflict to give her some warning, right?

"Mum," I said delicately. "What would happen if it turned out the person who killed Tessa... I mean, what if Tessa wasn't the murderer's first victim?"

"What?" Ramsey stared openly at me.

I paused for a moment, mentally bracing myself for the backlash. "Are you sure Grandma died of natural causes?"

Mum dropped my sleeve, her eyes blazing with fury. "I can't believe you'd say such a thing."

"Whoa." I took a step back in case she stabbed me with a needle, accidentally or otherwise. "It's bad enough someone killed poor Tessa, but you know, I wasn't around when Grandma died, and the timing seems suspicious from an outsider's perspective."

"She died in her sleep," Mum said firmly. "I used a spell myself to determine if any foul play had been involved. And that's the last I'll say on the matter."

I gave Ramsey a quizzical look, but he avoided my gaze. Typical. Yet I couldn't think of how else to interpret her paranoid behaviour, especially as some of it had begun before Tessa had died. Like dismissing the household staff, for instance.

"Just wondering." I yelped when she pulled the robe over my head with one hand, causing the pins to snag in my hair. "Ow."

"Sorry." She didn't meet my eyes. "I'll get this adjusted to the right size. If I were you, Robin, I'd go and ask your cousin for the details about what you have to do during the ceremony."

I assumed she meant Vanessa, but over my dead body was I asking for *her* advice. Instead, I shook off the sense of unease her words had left me with and headed for the house next door.

6

The last thing I wanted was to put myself in the path of Aunt Shannon again, but I knew how to find my younger cousin without coming into contact with the rest of her family. Instead of heading for the front door, I ducked down the alley that ran between our two houses before imitating the call of a blackbird.

For a moment, I wondered if she'd forgotten our signal. Then the topmost window slid open, and Rowan stuck her head out. "Quick, get up here before my mum notices."

Was her worry rooted in her old paranoia about the times Aunt Shannon had caught me climbing up to visit her and had punished both of us—or did she share my suspicions about the timing of Grandma's death? I climbed onto the fence and shimmied awkwardly up the drainpipe before reaching for the window ledge and pulling myself through into Rowan's room. It was a considerably tighter fit than it'd been when we were kids, but I managed to wriggle through in a manoeuvre Tansy would have been proud of and landed in a crouch on the carpet.

Rowan's room hadn't changed much in the years I'd been gone. The back wall was covered in tanks containing various bugs and reptiles, while Ralph the tarantula's web occupied an entire corner of the room. A large TV dominated the front of the room with her various games console systems. We'd spent many a happy all-nighter playing games up here as kids with soundproofed spells on the walls to stop Aunt Shannon from coming to yell at us for making too much noise. I could even vaguely remember a time when Ramsey had joined us too.

"I wondered what you were up to," she said. "I saw my mum going into your house earlier. Was she bothering you?"

"She was more intent on pestering *my* mum," I said. "Wanted to know about the plans for the coven leadership ceremony. That was when my mother volunteered me to take Tessa's place, and she told me to come and ask you for tips, so here I am."

Her brow shot up. "She wanted you to get advice from me?"

"Well, she probably meant your sister, but I don't want to talk to her."

A grin came to her mouth. "Sure, I can give you some pointers. Don't trip."

"Very funny," I said. "So I just have to carry the sceptre?"

"Essentially," she said. "It's a waste of time, really. They could have anyone do it, as long as they're capable of not tripping over their feet."

"Glad that cloak is being resized, then."

"She has you wearing Tessa's cloak?"

"What?" My skin prickled. "I hope not."

"Wouldn't surprise me," said Rowan. "Beats the hassle of buying a new one."

I grimaced and sat down on one of the giant beanbags. "Hope Tessa's luck doesn't rub off on me, then. Is your mum being even worse than usual this week?"

"She's a veritable nightmare," said Rowan. "Grandma's death pushed her over the edge. We had a screaming argument about her wanting to paint my room black like the rest of the house. I know it's temporary, but she doesn't get to touch my stuff."

"Wow," I said. "Mum only did it to the downstairs floor of our house, and it still looks like a low-budget horror movie. When was the last time you saw Grandma, anyway?"

I knew better than to expect Aunt Shannon to drop any hints about whether she suspected her mother's death hadn't been natural, but I was curious as to whether Rowan might have noticed anything odd.

"Ah... maybe the day before she died?" she said. "I don't remember. She was always busy."

"Yeah," I said. "I find it weird how everyone said she was fine, right up until she wasn't."

"That's usually how it is," she said. "Same with my dad. Fine one day, dead the next."

Uncle Les had been a terrible parent even by our coven's standards, forever disappearing for months at a time and generally being neglectful of his kids. Aunt Shannon hadn't shed a tear when he'd died and had remained seemingly oblivious to the rumours that she'd had him bumped off herself, and while Rowan had never seemed that bothered by the rumours, I didn't need to drag the mood down any further.

"I know Grandma was a workaholic," I said. "My mother's the same, and I can tell it's bugging her that she's having to postpone the ceremony. There doesn't seem to be a way around it, though, with half the coven in questioning by the police."

"Your brother thinks Tessa's killer might be among the coven members?" said Rowan. "He hasn't questioned me yet, but I guess he's going in order of importance."

"That'd make me the highest priority." I tried for a smile but didn't quite succeed. "He questioned me first so he could hurry me away from the scene. I think I got off lightly, all things considered."

"I bet." She furrowed her brow. "He questioned *you?*"

"And your mother. She told me." I'd guess he hadn't got to Vanessa and Rowan yet. "I'm struggling to see who Tessa, of all people, managed to annoy badly enough for them to kill her at the Head Witch's funeral."

Rowan's gaze dropped. "Maybe she saw or heard something she shouldn't have."

"Like what?" Had *she* known whether Grandma's death hadn't been an accident?

She shrugged. "No idea. Why was she hiding in the maze to begin with?"

"I guessed to get away from the crowd," I said. "Speaking of which, the Henbane Coven wants the maze themselves."

"Oh, yeah, Tiffany wanted to know if your mum would be keeping it," she said. "I can't believe she had the nerve to ask you at the funeral of all places. She's shameless."

Had the Henbane witches killed Tessa in order to get their territory back from our coven? Leaving a dead body in the maze was certainly one way to convince us to give it up, but even the Henbane Coven wouldn't go that far. Would they?

"Do any of the Henbane witches want the Head Witch title?" I asked.

"Who doesn't?" she said. "I bet they're scheming away now that they know they have an extra day to plan."

"Not much they can do to change the outcome, though," I said. "The sceptre picks whoever it wants."

The Head Witch was chosen by forces which weren't under anyone's control, and if Tiffany thought she could make the sceptre pick her, she might as well have tried to move the stars in the sky.

Rowan dropped her gaze, teeth running over her bottom lip. "Guess so."

Something was definitely bugging her, but nothing she'd said had suggested she had the same suspicions as I did, and I didn't want to tell her without proof in case a certain magpie was watching us. "How long did it take you to escape the funeral? I didn't see you in the grounds."

"I was avoiding my mother." She lifted her head. "Also, Vanessa told me you left with a strange man."

"Harvey." I gladly seized on the change of subject. "We were in the same class at school. He now plays Sky Hopper professionally."

"Ooh, him?" Her eyes gleamed knowingly. "You had a raging crush on him, I remember."

"I was fifteen." Given the incident with the coffee and the reporters, I doubted he thought of me as anything more than a klutz. "I'm not going to be here for long, though."

I intended to be out of town by the end of the week, and I didn't need to get distracted by a hot guy. Besides, if Mum realised that she might be able to get me set up with one of the locals, she might end up adding it to her arsenal of arguments in order to convince me to stay. I did not want Harvey to become an unintentional pawn in my family's games.

Rowan looked slightly deflated, but she revived when Vanessa opened the bedroom door and sidled into the room. "Thought I heard your voice, Robin."

Rowan scowled at her older sister. "What do you want?"

"I'm told I need to tell Robin how to carry the sceptre to the coven leadership ceremony to make sure she doesn't screw up."

So much for keeping it quiet. "Who told you that?"

"My mum did," she said. "She said you were taking Tessa's place."

Thanks for that, Aunt Shannon. "Look, I'm pretty sure I can walk in a straight line and carry a sceptre. I don't need any pointers."

"I'd have thought you'd have helped at the ceremony at least once before," she said. "I suppose Grandma knew you wouldn't be any use at it, same as everything else."

"I don't see anyone falling over themselves to offer *you* the job." Okay, Mum had threatened to ask Vanessa in my place if I'd said no, but I'd bet Aunt Shannon was fuming that I'd said yes. "What makes you the expert?"

"I've actually paid attention to my coven for the last

few years." She stepped closer until we stood nose to nose, while my temper frayed at the edges.

Behind my back, I heard Rowan whisper something under her breath. Then a scuttling noise made me spin around in time to see Ralph the tarantula swing from his web and crash straight into Vanessa's face.

Vanessa waved her hands around, trying to knock the spider away, but he moved too fast to be caught. She let out a shrill yelp when Ralph ran over the back of her head, leaving a trail of cobwebs behind him. "Call him off!"

"Only if you get out of my room." Rowan beckoned, and Ralph scuttled back to his owner when Vanessa backed into the doorway. "I thought you were supposed to be giving Robin advice, not acting like a brat."

"I'm not the one who can't keep her familiar under control." Vanessa swept a hand over the back of her head in an attempt to get rid of the cobwebs. "If you screw this up, Robin, then our whole coven will be the laughingstock of the magical world."

"I already heard that from *my* mother, but go on, give me your words of wisdom." I gave her an expectant look. "Or were you expecting me to hand over the responsibility to you instead?"

"I don't see why not," said Vanessa. "*I* never ran away from town when my family needed me."

They didn't need me. "If you missed me so badly, you might have sent me a postcard."

Rowan snickered. "Yeah, leaving town isn't a crime. Maybe I want to do the same, in fact."

Vanessa narrowed her eyes at her sister. "Mum would never allow it. She'd disown you first."

Rowan took a step back, a flush creeping up her neck. "She isn't going to be Head Witch, Vanessa. And nor are you."

It was Vanessa's turn to flush. "Says who? The whole process of selecting the Head Witch is ridiculous, if you ask me. As if a ceremonial sceptre can have a clue how to judge the worthiest candidate."

"It *is* a powerful magical object," I pointed out, more in an attempt to defuse the tension than anything else. "The process has worked for this long, hasn't it?"

Vanessa sniffed. "I can't believe even *you* believe in that nonsense."

"Shouldn't I?" It was no secret that I thought pretty much everything the coven did was several centuries out of date, but not even Aunt Shannon would dream of overturning such an important tradition. Right?

Vanessa gave me a withering look. "I thought you said other magical communities had different approaches."

"Yes, with picking their coven leader," I corrected. "Head Witch, though… that's a whole other matter, and I doubt anyone wants to rock the boat right after losing Grandma. And after a murder at her funeral too."

"Murder?" She snorted. "Hardly. The girl probably fell into the fountain by accident."

"Is that what you think?"

Vanessa gave a shrug, not quite meeting my eyes. "It doesn't matter. The truth will never come out, considering who's in charge of the questioning."

"And why's that?" What was she talking about? "My brother is dedicated to his job. He'll be sure to question everyone carefully to get at the truth."

She laughed. "Do you really believe that? He'd overturn justice to protect his close family in a heartbeat, and don't you even think he wouldn't. If your mother told him to quit his job right now, he would. I guarantee it."

Huh? "She's not going to ask him to quit his job."

Ramsey might have been obedient to a fault, but he wouldn't give up the position he'd worked so hard to earn. Not even if Mum asked him to. He wouldn't hide the results of an investigation, either. No, Vanessa was just trying to get under my skin. And succeeding. Was she really that mad at me for taking Tessa's place, or did she actually know something about her death that she hadn't told my brother?

"I guess you've been away for long enough that you missed a lot," Vanessa went on. "Did your mother mention she and Grandma had an argument the night before she died?"

I stared openly at her for a moment. "How'd you know that?"

"I heard them," she said. "They were outside your house, and I had the window open at the time. I didn't catch what they were saying, but they sounded pretty mad at one another."

"And?" I studied her expression, which lingered somewhere between angry and mocking. "They argued all the time, same as Grandma and *your* mum."

"Except they didn't make up this time, because Grandma was dead by morning."

She couldn't be implying what I thought she was. "Grandma died in her sleep."

"That's what the official story says, but it was your mum who found her, wasn't it?"

Vanessa thought Grandma's death hadn't been an accident. Did she think my *mother* had killed Grandma? Or was this an attempt to deflect attention from her own side of the family? Aunt Shannon was the person with the most unsavoury rumours attached to her, but I hadn't thought she'd go as far as to commit murder.

Rowan gaped open-mouthed at her without saying a word, clearly as stunned as I was at her sister's outburst.

"The official story says Tessa was murdered," I said through gritted teeth. "We were talking about her, not Grandma. My brother wouldn't be questioning the entire council if he didn't believe her death wasn't an accident."

Mum couldn't have had anything to do with Tessa's death. She hadn't been anywhere near the maze at the time and had been surrounded by a crowd for the entire funeral. As for Grandma, Mum had been her biggest admirer and had ultimately found herself having to be the one to handle the fallout from her death. Postponing the ceremony was the opposite of what Mum had wanted.

Yes, she'd shot down my suggestion that Tessa's death hadn't been an accident, but who could blame her? All the coven's attention was on her, and she was due to be confirmed as the next Head Witch and coven leader tomorrow. The last thing she needed was her authority to be undermined by rumours nobody could confirm.

"It hardly matters one way or another," Vanessa said. "The sceptre will pick the person it considers worthy. You'd better hope the cards fall in your favour."

"I told you to get out of my room." Rowan's hands curled into fists. "Go on."

A commotion rose from outside the window behind me, cawing noises mingling with the shuffling crash which sounded like a bird falling off a wall. I veered in that direction, my heart swooping at the sight of several black-and-white feathers falling out of sight. *That magpie!*

"Tansy?" I stuck my head out the window, seeing her fluffy red tail sticking up from the fence below. "Was that Myrtle?"

"Get out!" Rowan yelled from behind me, and the scuttling sound of a dozen spiders converging on her sister filled the background.

I didn't stick around to see the fallout. Climbing onto the windowsill, I reached upward to pull myself outside and got halfway out before I ended up stuck. I wriggled, upside-down, while Tansy perched on the fence and laughed at me.

"A little help would be nice."

There wasn't much my familiar could do to extract me from the window, though, so I had to keep wriggling until I'd freed myself and then scramble into an upright position to climb down the drainpipe. Breathless, I hopped over the fence into the alleyway, where no signs remained of my aunt's magpie familiar except a few feathers. "Was Myrtle eavesdropping?"

"Not for long," Tansy said. "I caught her in the act."

"Good." I leaned on the fence to catch my breath, my mind still reeling from Vanessa's cutting words. "Aunt Shannon sent Vanessa to hassle Rowan and me, so I should have figured she'd keep an eye on us."

"What did she do that for?"

"Mum pressured me to ask Vanessa to get tips for taking Tessa's place at the ceremony, so I paid Rowan a visit instead," I explained. "Speaking of which, I have a bone to pick with her about making me wear Tessa's robes."

"She wants you to wear the outfit Tessa died in?"

"I'm guessing she couldn't get a replacement in time," I said. "Maybe it's a weird thing to kick up a fuss about, but she might have mentioned it earlier."

"I'd say not," she said. "You agreed to Tessa's place, though? What did she bribe you with?"

"Nobody mentioned bribery." My familiar's knowing look told me she wasn't fooled. "All right, she said she'd buy me that camera."

Tansy groaned. "*You* said you wouldn't stay."

"I'm not staying, I'm doing a last-minute favour for the coven," I said. "Anyway, you like it here, don't you? You've been having a whale of a time in the garden all day."

"I don't want to stay here if *you* don't like it." She sat on the fence, her bushy tail sticking straight up in the air.

"That isn't the problem." I'd have been lying if I said being near the Wildwood again didn't make my magic feel like it was functioning again for the first time in years, but if the price I had to pay was running around doing favours for the coven, I wasn't entirely sure it was worth the trade-off. Especially if it put me on the radar of a murderer. On the other hand, the notion of turning my back at a time like this wasn't appealing, either. Not until I knew for sure if Grandma's death hadn't been an accident.

And if Vanessa of all people believed otherwise, how many other members of my family agreed? Was Mum's firm shutdown of the subject due to her suspicion that someone in our own family might have played a part in her death? Had she told Ramsey? I didn't believe for an instant that he'd cover for a murderer, even if a member of the family had been involved, but if Vanessa had simply been trying to unnerve me, she'd certainly succeeded.

Honestly. If anyone would use any means to get what they wanted, it was Aunt Shannon. She might even have asked Vanessa to do her dirty work for her and then try to deflect attention by pinning the blame on Mum.

Tansy studied my face. "Are you okay?"

"Have you seen that magpie anywhere else?" I asked. "Like in the garden?"

"No," she said. "Oh, I think I saw her flying towards the coven's headquarters earlier…"

"Is anyone even there?" I emerged from the alley, my gaze travelling across the road towards the coven's headquarters. The building was so vast that it dwarfed the smaller property next door, which belonged to the Henbane Coven. "I hope they kept the maze warded against intruders at least."

"Of course they did," Tansy said. "Why?"

"The Henbane Coven," I said. "They still have their sights set on owning that maze. Tiffany told me at the funeral, before we found Tessa's body."

Her beady eyes gleamed. "I can go and snoop over the fence if you like."

"Not yet." But her words had given me an idea. "If Aunt Shannon is going to send her magpie to spy on us, though, I wouldn't mind returning the favour."

"You want me to spy on her?" she asked.

"Only if you don't get caught." I kept my voice low. "I think Aunt Shannon is scheming to become Head Witch herself, and I'm pretty sure Vanessa's in on it too."

Whether they'd taken out the last Head Witch in the process I didn't know, but it'd set my mind at ease to know someone was keeping an eye on them.

"Gotcha." She leapt across the fence to the neighbouring house and began scaling the drainpipe. I watched her, unsure if I shouldn't have sent her to spy on the Henbane Coven instead. They certainly had a good reason to want the Head Witch's title, but Vanessa's accusations had wormed their way under my skin. Why would she blame my mother if not to deflect attention from her own?

"Robin." Mum's voice whipped out at me from the doorstep of the house. "Get in here."

Oh, boy. She must still have been mad at me for implying Grandma's death hadn't been an accident.

Taking in a breath, I approached the house to meet her. "Were you planning to tell me I'll be wearing Tessa's cloak to the ceremony?"

"She doesn't have any use for it herself, does she?"

My mouth parted. "That's kinda harsh, Mum."

Vanessa's words came to mind again, and a shiver of unease ran down my spine. I didn't believe my cousin. Mum was under a lot of stress, and I probably hadn't helped by voicing her worst fears about her predecessor's fate.

Her lips compressed. "The robes are custom-made, and if Tessa was here, she wouldn't mind you borrowing them."

"I was just making an observation."

I didn't believe Vanessa. I *didn't*. But the mere thought of mentioning her taunts to Mum made the words stick in my throat. Did Mum have the faintest idea that her sister and niece were spreading rumours about her involvement in her predecessor's death? Mum must suspect her sister had her sights set on becoming Head Witch, at the very least.

Mum took a step backwards into the hall. "I'll adjust

the robes by tomorrow. Do try to stay out of trouble before then, won't you?"

"I thought you wanted me to come in the house." Was she acting weirdly, or was my own paranoia colouring my every observation? "Isn't there a dress rehearsal for tomorrow?"

"Not with half the coven still in questioning," she said. "You're free for the rest of the day."

"I am?" Not that I was complaining, but my encounter with my cousins had knocked me off-balance and made me forget everything else I'd intended to do while I was still in town.

I fished my mobile phone out of my pocket and sent a message to my best friend, Piper. As long as I was here, I might as well make the most of the best that Wildwood Heath had to offer.

7

Piper responded to my message with an enthusiastic yes, so I met her at the local pub, the Fox's Den, for a late lunch. I checked for any unwelcome reporters before going in, but the coast was clear. Maybe Clarice and Speck were still ambushing patrons at the café instead.

"Exciting week, isn't it?" Piper bounded into the pub behind me, her curly dark hair styled instead of tied back and the muddy gardening clothes she usually wore replaced by a skirt and a lacy blouse. Since she wasn't doing any gardening work for the coven at the moment, she must be having a positively relaxing week compared to mine.

"You might say that." I picked out a table by the window, and we both ordered bangers and mash, the dish of the day. "Mum gave me the rest of the day off, by some miracle, and I figured you'd be free."

"Yeah, since the future Head Witch banished me from the garden." She rolled her eyes. "She said I'm not to come back until Monday. I hope she's okay with her prize roses suffering until then."

"She's trying to take care of them herself, I think." Piper had been at the funeral, but as a minor coven member, she hadn't been on the high-priority list of people for my brother to question. Also, Mum wouldn't have dreamed of accusing her best gardener of committing a crime, even if she had dismissed the household staff for the time being. "Did she mention *why* she was giving you the week off?"

"Generosity?" She gave a shrug and picked up the cocktail menu. "It's not too early to get myself a marshberry whirl, is it?"

"I'd say not." I ordered a cocktail of my own by tapping the right order on the menu with my fingertip and settled back in my seat. "What've you been doing all week, then?"

"Aside from going to the funeral?" she asked. "Mostly, I've been turning down requests from the Henbane Coven to start working on *their* gardens. I had to explain I'm still working for your mother and that I haven't been fired."

"Seriously?" When a pair of neon-pink cocktails appeared on the table, I picked up my straw and gave mine a stir. "Did they mention why they want a gardener all of a sudden?"

"They probably want to get in on the flower contest next time." She sipped her cocktail. "Anyway, I'm not about to start drama by accepting work from a rival coven."

"No kidding." They hadn't wasted any time by asking me if Mum wanted to keep the maze, but I hadn't known they wanted to hire Grandma's gardener too. "You'll be at the ceremony tomorrow, right?"

"Wouldn't miss it," she said. "And you?"

"Yeah… I'm temporarily taking Tessa's place."

I launched into an explanation of the events of the last couple of days. Our food appeared on the table halfway through, and I dug into my meal with gusto as I told Piper about my encounters with the press, my unfortunate discovery of Tessa's body at the funeral, and then Mum's unexpected offer.

Piper shook her head. "I can't believe your mother roped you into staying. She does know you have a life of your own, doesn't she?"

"Yes, but I already committed to staying here all week," I said. "Granted, I was on the brink of leaving town after the funeral, but that plan flew out the window when I found Tessa's body. Mum's offered to buy me the camera I was saving for if I take Tessa's place. Hard to say no to that offer."

She chewed a mouthful of potato and swallowed. "I'd do the same. I'm not complaining about having my best friend back for the week, anyway."

Neither was I, despite the unfortunate circumstances. When we were teenagers, we'd spent hours at a time chatting in the garden while she worked her magic on Grandma's prizewinning rosebushes, and while we kept in touch via messages, it wasn't the same. As the coven's gardener, she was more plugged into gossip than me and knew virtually everything which had gone on behind the scenes up until Grandma's death and Mum's abrupt dismissal of her and the other staff.

"Was my aunt acting weirdly at all?" I asked her. "Or my grandmother?"

"Everyone in your family is weird. No offence."

"None taken." I sipped the dregs of my cocktail. "Everyone is on edge, that's all. How'd you find out my grandma died?"

"Your mum told me." She stirred the remainder of her drink, a thoughtful look on her face. "I showed up at the usual time, and she practically shut the door in my face. She said the Head Witch had died and ordered me not to tell anyone else. I imagine the secrecy lasted for all of five minutes before the entire coven knew."

I grimaced. "My cousin told me before Mum did. She was still mad at me after our last argument."

"Oh." She looked down at the menu and ordered another drink. "She's forgiven you now, right? She must have if she gave you Tessa's job."

"It was me or my cousin Vanessa."

"Oh, *her*." She pulled a face. "I saw her at the funeral. Her mother too. Were they hassling you?"

"Yep. Hence my escape into the maze."

She'd likely seen me almost lose control of my magic too. Aunt Shannon had been trying to push my buttons, but her attempt to humiliate me might have gone beyond her usual taunting if she was working behind the scenes to undermine my mother. I hoped she and Vanessa hadn't dropped hints to anyone else that the former Head Witch hadn't died by accident.

Another pair of cocktails appeared on the table, and Piper took a sip from hers. "Your aunt's a sore loser."

"She hasn't lost yet," I reminded her. "She has her sights set on the Head Witch title."

"She won't get it," Piper said confidently. "Come on, your mum's been tipped as the Head Witch's successor for years."

"True." Aunt Shannon always lost to her older sister, and it was no wonder she felt the need to resort to underhanded trickery. The sceptre would see right through her act. "The sooner the ceremony is over, the better."

The cosy pub seemed a world away from the coven's drama, and it was nice to chat about everything I'd missed when I hadn't been around without the fear of judgement. Piper would support me whether I stayed or left, and it was a relief not to have to justify every decision I made to her. My mood improved even more when Harvey walked into the pub with a group of athletic-looking people who I assumed also played for the local Sky Hopper team. When he caught my eye, I waved at him, while Piper followed my gaze. "That's Harvey, right? I didn't know you were in touch."

"We ran into one another twice in the last couple of days." I watched out of the corner of my eye as his group selected a table near ours and sat down. "Literally, the second time around."

"Ooh," she said. "Didn't you have a major crush on him at school?"

"I did." I kept my voice low, but the pub was noisy enough that we had to lean across the table to properly hear one another. "We hadn't spoken for years until he came to talk to me after the funeral and offered to walk me home, though."

"He did?" She practically bounced up and down in her seat. "Wow, maybe he felt the same as you did."

"Keep it down," I muttered. "Don't forget I'd just found a dead body and there was a potential killer on the loose."

"You said you ran into one another again... literally?"

Her eyes glittered with amusement. "How'd you manage that?"

"The press were hounding me at the coffee shop, so I made a hasty exit without looking where I was going."

She snorted. "Sorry, I shouldn't laugh. I saw them through the window when I walked past and decided to get my coffee elsewhere."

"Wise choice." My heart skipped a beat when I spotted Harvey approaching our table. "Hey."

"Are you here to watch the open-mic night?" he asked.

"I didn't know there was one," I said. "Piper and I were planning to stick around for a while, right?"

"Sure," said Piper, without hesitation. "And she's going to sing—"

I nudged her under the table. "I'm definitely not going to sing, but I figured I might as well check out the local entertainment while I'm free for the evening."

"You are?" His eyes brightened. "I thought you'd be doing stuff for the coven."

"That's tomorrow," I said. "The ceremony for the next Head Witch, I mean."

Besides, I could enjoy a little harmless flirtation while I made the most of my one night of freedom. I'd earned that much.

The evening passed pleasantly, and the longer I spent chatting with Piper and exchanging stories with Harvey's friends, the more I had to remind myself that I wasn't here forever. Even without taking my family responsibilities into account, Wildwood Heath had a habit of getting a hold over me and not letting go, and it went deeper than our family's magical connection to nature.

Speaking of family. I looked over at the door in a lull

during the open-mic event and was stunned to see my brother, of all people, entering the pub. Had Ramsey taken the night off for the first time in the decade since he'd joined the police force? Maybe he had, but his expression was as serious as ever when he zeroed in on our table.

Piper goggled at him from opposite me. "What's he doing here?"

"Hey." I waved him over. "Come and join us."

Ramsey walked to our table, but he stood stiffly at my side instead of sitting down. "Is this really an appropriate place for you to be spending your time?"

"Lighten up," I said. "It's not like I'm obligated to stay at home."

Yes, the Fox's Den didn't belong to the coven and was run by shifters instead, but that was *why* I liked it. Being around non-witches enabled a degree of anonymity which came from not constantly running into people who were only acquainted with me as Roxanne Wildwood's daughter.

Ramsey inched closer to my chair and lowered his voice. "I would prefer you didn't get us into any more trouble."

"What kind of trouble?" I genuinely had no idea what he was talking about, since it wasn't as if I'd had the chance to mess up the ceremony yet.

"Someone," he said, through clenched teeth, "ratted us out to the press."

I choked on the sip of my drink I'd just taken. "Who?"

"You tell me," he said. "Since they knew things which only someone in our family could have told them."

"I didn't tell them a thing," I said. "Come on, you know I wouldn't do that."

"It wouldn't be the first time."

That was unfortunately true, but I'd have preferred not to have this conversation in here. My brother could suck the fun out of a room just by stepping into it. Piper's eyes were as round as saucers, and while Harvey hadn't spotted the new arrival yet, I needed to get him out of here before he deflated our entire evening like a pin puncturing a balloon.

"Sorry." I rose to my feet. "I'll be back in a second."

I hurried out of the pub behind Ramsey, the cold evening air as much of a shock as his accusation. *I can't believe he said that.* The question was, who had spoken to the press if not me?

Once we were out of earshot of anyone inside the pub, I rotated on my heel to face him. "Are you kidding me?"

"No, I'm definitely not kidding," he said. "The *Blue Moon* has an article on their website full of speculation that the former Head Witch was murdered."

My throat went dry. "Even if I'd said anything to them, I definitely wouldn't have told anyone *that*. What did the article say?"

"Read it yourself." He pushed his phone in front of my face, but the article's words danced in front of my eyes and refused to make any sense. Except, that is, for the two names at the top of the screen.

"Clarice and Speck." I swore under my breath. "They were hanging around the coffee shop earlier and tried to ambush me, but I didn't say a word to them."

"Did they follow you? Or stick a microphone on you?"

"Even if they had, it'd have gone straight in the wash

when I changed out of my clothes to try on those robes," I pointed out. "I might add that I also spilled coffee all over myself trying to get away from them. Are you sure Aunt Shannon and Vanessa aren't setting me up to take the blame?"

Mum's fury when I'd hinted that her mother's death hadn't been accidental had meant I hadn't got close to asking *her* for her perspective on the argument between herself and Grandma the night before the Head Witch's death, but that didn't mean there was a grain of truth in Vanessa's accusations.

"Nobody is setting you up," Ramsey said firmly.

"Then why don't you believe me?" He might have been under pressure to solve the case, but ruining my night by making baseless accusations was a step too far. "I have nothing to gain from trashing our family's reputation by blabbing to reporters. Nothing whatsoever."

"I'm sure you didn't *mean* to give anything away, but you're known for speaking without thinking," he said. "Like that interview you did with the *Blue Moon* a few years ago."

"I was a kid who didn't know any better," I reminded him. "Besides, we weren't dealing with a murder at the time. I think you're missing the big picture here."

Did he seriously think I'd choose *now* to start spreading rumours which might put the rest of the family in danger?

"*I'm* missing the big picture?" he said. "You've been neglecting your responsibilities from the start."

Anger sparked, and my magic started to fizzle in my fingertips. The sound of bird wings fluttering overhead warned me that if I didn't get control over my temper,

Ramsey would have yet another reason to drag me back home. I curled my hands into fists and took in a deep breath. "If you want the truth, then go in there and ask Harvey. I ran into him at the café when I was escaping the press, and he can tell you exactly what I told them."

He frowned. "Who?"

"Harvey," I said. "You do remember I told you he's captain of the Sky Hopper team, right?"

"He walked you home after the funeral." Suspicion flared in his eyes. "He's not with the coven."

"Yes, so he has nothing to gain from making excuses for me," I said. "We knew one another at school, that's all."

"Did *he* speak to the press?" he asked. "You shouldn't talk about the coven's business with outsiders."

"No." I threw up my hands. "Good lord, you're paranoid. We have plenty to talk about that isn't remotely related to the coven."

If he started trying to police my social life as well as accusing me of lying, then he was barking up the wrong tree.

Ramsey watched through narrowed eyes as a group of drunken wizards walked past. "When you're here in Wildwood Heath, everything you do reflects back on the coven one way or another."

I raised a brow. "If you're truly so concerned, then feel free to come and join us and watch the open-mic night. You might even enjoy it."

"I have responsibilities," he said.

"Like accusing your sister of gossiping about our family." I did my best to swallow down my lingering anger, keeping my voice even. "Word of advice? I'd save the accusations for the members of our family who actually want the title of Head Witch."

"I can't believe you're still defying our mother at a time like this."

"She told me to do as I wanted this evening," I said. "Besides, shouldn't doing your job and finding the killer take precedence over trying to save the family's public image?"

His face reddened. "*What* did you say?"

I'd gone too far, I knew, but the two cocktails I'd drunk had washed away my inhibitions, and his accusation had flung a final spark onto the flame of my frustrations at my family. "Vanessa told me earlier that Mum was the last person to talk to the Head Witch before she died. Did she mention that when you questioned her?"

His face went from red to maroon, and for a moment, I wondered if my brother would lose his tightly honed control over his magic. His closed expression tightened even further. "If I hear you've done anything more to damage our reputation tonight, then I'll personally see to it that you're removed from tomorrow's ceremony altogether."

He turned his back and left without another word. Several blackbirds fluttered down, surrounding me, drawn to the magic sparking from my palms... and to the trail of anger Ramsey had left behind him.

"As if," I muttered. "I bet Vanessa was the one who blabbed to the press. She at least has a reason to screw with our reputation."

He was too far away to hear my reply, of course, so I returned to the pub and did my level best to forget my brother's accusations. He might have wrecked my mood, but he'd reminded me of why I had zero intention of sticking around after this week.

No matter how nice it was to hang out with Piper and flirt with Harvey, I had to remember I didn't belong here. I had a life of my own, and nobody—not the press and not my family—would take it from me.

8

"**O**uch." I pulled the covers over my head as the brightness of the ceiling light dazzled my eyes. "I may have had one drink too many last night."

"Told you so," said Tansy's voice from nearby.

"You didn't," I mumbled. "You weren't there."

"I've told you before," she said. "Consider my advice to apply to every time you go out drinking. It saves me repeating myself."

"It doesn't happen *that* often."

She jumped on the bed, and I groaned when the mattress shook under her excited bouncing. "No, but you have past experience to tell you how it usually ends."

I thought back to the previous night. I hadn't said anything too outrageous, had I? There'd been my spat with Ramsey, but he'd accused me of spreading lies about our family to the press. Honestly, he was equally to blame for my hangover, considering it'd taken two more cocktails to bring my mood back to its former level. "Hey, at least I made it home."

"Not by yourself," she said. "I'm willing to bet someone had to carry you."

"Nice to know you have faith in me." I peered at Tansy from under the covers, but even the faintest sliver of light was too much for my sensitive eyes. "What time is it?"

"Late enough that the coven leadership vote is already underway."

"Oh, no." I sat bolt upright, triggering a wave of nausea that made my head spin. I closed my eyes and gripped both sides of the bed until it passed, and when I opened them again, my gaze landed on a small potion bottle on the bedside table. "What's that?"

Tansy gave the bottle a sniff. "I believe it's a hangover cure."

"Huh." Had Harvey given it to me before I'd left? I doubted my brother had, so it must have been him or Piper. Without hesitation, I downed the whole thing in one go, and my raging headache began to subside almost at once. "Who gave me this, did you see?"

"Haven't a clue," she said. "Have you forgotten I was spying on that unpleasant cousin of yours while you were gone?"

"That's right." I climbed out of bed, no longer bothered by the bright sunlight. "Did you hear anything interesting?"

"No," she said. "Unless you count Vanessa and her mother calculating how many votes they needed to get between them in order to snag the coven leadership."

"What?" I pressed my hand to my forehead. "Oh. I forgot Vanessa was on the council as well."

If she surrendered her own votes to Aunt Shannon, it'd add an edge to the competition. That wouldn't stop Mum from winning if enough people chose her, of course, but I couldn't believe I'd forgotten Vanessa had joined the coven's council alongside her mother. Not that I'd be able to do anything to change the outcome, since I wasn't on the council myself and hadn't even been invited to the meeting which would determine who took the position.

The meeting itself was more of a formality, since the members of the council rarely changed their minds at the last minute. Once each person in the running for leadership had given a quick speech, then every council member cast an anonymous vote for the person they thought most fit to run the coven for the next term of leadership. Nobody knew anyone else's votes before the results were revealed, and Aunt Shannon would have a hard job manipulating the vote under the eyes of some of the most powerful witches in town. But that didn't mean she wouldn't try.

"Tansy," I said, "can you go to the witches' headquarters and make sure that magpie isn't lurking anywhere she isn't supposed to be?"

"With pleasure." She skittered across the room and out the partially open window, while I checked the time and groaned quietly when I realised I had less than an hour until the formal ceremony was due to start. My phone's battery was dead, so I plugged it in and found an array of jumbled messages from the previous night, mostly from a very drunk Piper. She'd also sent me a link to the article which had got Ramsey so worked up.

I sat down on the bed with another groan. If Ramsey

had told tales on me to Mum, I wouldn't be in for a major tongue-lashing until after the ceremony was over, so at least I had that much in my favour.

Skimming the article on my phone left me with a headache almost as bad as my hangover, though. Clarice and Speck had struck gold with whoever they'd chosen to interview, as they'd shared everything from the speculation on the death of the former Head Witch to the possibility that one of her own family members had been involved in her murder. To add insult to injury, they also knew I was set to take Tessa's place. Outside of the family, I'd only told Piper and Harvey, and I hadn't mentioned it to them until after the article had already been printed. Did Ramsey seriously think I'd paint a target on my own head on purpose? He must know Aunt Shannon and Vanessa had been responsible.

For a brief moment, I was tempted to bunk off the ceremony altogether, but imagining the smirk on Aunt Shannon's face if I never showed up was enough to squash that impulse. I shut off the article and went to get ready for the ceremony.

When I put on Tessa's robes, I found they'd at least been resized to fit me, even if they did belong to a dead woman. Regardless, my legs were restless, and I had no appetite for breakfast even after my hangover cure. Stage fright wasn't usually my thing, but I found myself glad the ceremony would take place indoors. If I lost control of my magic, the odds of being interrupted by a flock of seagulls were lower than if we'd been out in the open.

With fifteen minutes to go, I left the house and walked the short distance to the coven's headquarters. The entire lobby remained ominously quiet as I crept through to wait in the back garden for the verdict. Other coven members filled the back garden, dressed in formal wear for the ceremony, and I skirted the paved area to avoid drawing attention. Rowan ought to be here, but I didn't see my youngest cousin anywhere.

As I sat down to wait on a bench, Tansy came running into view. "I chased that magpie off the roof," she said. "I think she was trying to spy on the meeting through the windows, not cheat, but it's better to be sure."

"True." It'd be near impossible for Aunt Shannon to circumvent the eagle-eyed witches on the council, and the voting rules were stringent enough to prevent bribery and magical coercion from influencing anyone's choices. Hence why cancelling or delaying the event would have been the only way to prevent a new leader from being chosen, and even Tessa's murder had only pushed the event forward by a day.

Not being able to see what was going on inside the building made me edgy, so I paced along the gap between the fence and the whitewashed wall while holding my robes off the ground so that I didn't trip.

"Are you wearing Baby Yoda socks?" Tansy snickered.

"Quiet," I murmured. "You're okay. You don't need to wear silly outfits *or* attend the ceremony."

I wished it was socially acceptable for me to run over the fences and climb trees to blow off steam like Tansy did, but even she was more hyper and jittery than usual. No doubt my nerves were rubbing off on her. I forced my pacing feet to a halt near the paved area in front of the building, and my heart swooped downward when I spotted my brother exiting the coven's headquarters. He didn't so much as glance in my direction, and I wouldn't lie, I was relieved to postpone our inevitable awkward confrontation. By now, almost every coven member who wasn't on the council waited outside. Had Ramsey been questioning someone? He must have been. My brother would never dare risk being late for the ceremony without a good reason. Unless he'd gone out and got drunk last night as well, but that was as likely as him joining the circus.

Maybe he found out who leaked our secrets to the press. If he had ambushed Vanessa and Aunt Shannon in front of an audience, I'd be tempted to forgive him for last night's accusations for the sheer entertainment value. The press, of course, had been barred from the entire building, so they could only speculate on what was going on in there.

Minutes passed in a tense silence before the twin oak doors swung open and Mum strode outside. Everyone held their breaths at once for a long moment, until Mum raised her voice so that the entire garden could hear. 'I have been offered the position of the Wildwood Coven's new leader, and I have chosen to accept the title."

Did I detect a little relief in her tone? Maybe, but the unknotting of tension in my own chest took me by surprise. The murmur of acknowledgement that passed among the other witches suggested most of them agreed, and as the tension eased, I felt the bizarre impulse to do a celebratory dance when it hit me that at least I didn't have to hand the sceptre to Aunt Shannon. If anyone noticed a dozen birds in the nearby trees spontaneously burst into song, they didn't say.

"Come in." Mum's gaze was on me, and I heard her unspoken words: *Don't screw this up, Robin.*

Here we go. I followed her through the door to the

coven's meeting room. The rows of seats facing the platform at the front hadn't moved since the funeral, but in the place where Grandma's coffin had been was a clear case containing the ceremonial sceptre.

The rest of the council already occupied most of the seats in front of the dais, while I took a seat in my usual spot and did my best not to look at my brother. The rest of the coven's members filled out the seats behind me, though I didn't see Rowan among them. Maybe she had a hangover too. Or she'd slept in. Both were equally likely, but I found my thoughts going back to her argument with her sister the previous day. Vanessa sat beside her mother, looking tired and crabby, and her lips pursed when Mum took the stage. Satisfaction straightened my back, and piano music played from speakers as Mum walked up to the stage and took up her position on the dais.

Everyone stood and clapped at the same time until the music petered out and Mum began her speech.

"Ordinarily, the region's Head Witch would do the honour of presenting the new leader of the Wildwood Coven with their title," said Mum. "However, the council came to a mutual decision to cast our votes for the coven's leader before the new Head Witch is chosen. I am delighted to announce that I have accepted the position."

Everyone clapped, the mood notably brighter than earlier. Everything was proceeding as planned, which meant the era of uncertainty which had lingered since Grandma's death would soon come to an end. Mum would remain coven leader until the next election, in contrast to the position of Head Witch, which renewed annually and was chosen at complete random. Yet there didn't seem to be any doubt in the room that Mum would take both titles.

Here we go.

My heartbeat quickened as her gaze landed on me, the slightest gesture indicating for me to stand up. Holding my breath, I rose to my feet and walked forwards until I reached the dais. Then I lifted the ceremonial sceptre out of its glass case and presented it to my mother.

Despite my sweaty palms, I kept hold of the long, carved instrument until it safely lay on top of the pedestal in front of the room.

A glow sprang to the sceptre's end, startling me so that I almost tripped off the stage. Had it started reacting to someone already? Was it about to choose a new Head Witch?

"Robin," my brother hissed from the front row. "Get over here."

I returned to my seat and sat down, but I couldn't take my eyes off the glowing instrument. I wasn't the only one who'd noticed. Several gasps broke out in the rows behind me, while the rest of the council members rose to their feet.

Mum stood behind the pedestal, her expression calm. "It seems the time has come for a new Head Witch to be chosen."

She reached for the sceptre, but before her fingers could close around its end, the sceptre leapt into the air as if drawn by an invisible force. A collective gasp rose throughout the room. Instead of landing in Mum's hands as everyone had expected, the instrument remained hovering above our heads and began to spin like the point of a compass. Its purplish light passed over the rows of attendees before focusing on a single person.

Grandma.

Her stooped figure stood in the aisle as if she was simply a guest who'd shown up late, oblivious to the ripple of shock that passed through the room when the others realised who the sceptre had pointed to. Grandma reached out a hand, transparent as a thinly spun web.

Several people screamed, while Aunt Shannon leapt to her feet in the front row. "What is going on?"

The sceptre floated downward, and my heart jumped into my throat. As Grandma's fingers reached for the sceptre, they simply passed straight through the end as if it didn't exist.

"She's a ghost!" gasped someone who was slower on the uptake than the rest of us.

More screams echoed throughout, while someone in the back row sank out of her seat into a dead faint.

Mum, to her credit, met the ghost's eyes calmly. "Mother, you can't take the sceptre. You're dead."

"I beg to differ." Grandma wasn't standing in the aisle but floating unsupported above the ground, yet the old stubbornness in her tone gave me an uncanny feeling.

It's really her.

"The sceptre can't choose a ghost as its wielder," Mum insisted.

As far as I knew, that was true. Yet why had the sceptre pointed towards her? Did it somehow still recognise Grandma as its wielder, even from beyond the grave? She had certainly *tried* to grab the instrument, growing more visibly impatient when her transparent hand failed to get a grip on it.

Ramsey watched her with an expression of mounting horror on his face, but I didn't have the slightest urge to laugh at him. None of us had foreseen an interruption from the former Head Witch's ghost. Had someone summoned her restless spirit, or had she risen of her own accord? Several of the council members left their seats and reached for the sceptre, but a flash of light from the instrument sent them reeling backwards.

In the shocked silence that followed, Grandma rotated on the spot and vanished into thin air. The sceptre fell to earth with a deafening clang which made everyone in the room jump.

"Nobody touch that!" With a wave of her wand, Mum levitated the sceptre back into its glass case. "Leave the sceptre until I say otherwise."

This might have been the first new Head Witch ceremony in several decades, but I had an inkling that being interrupted by the ghost of the sceptre's previous wielder wasn't a common occurrence. The Head Witch had been wildly popular, but nobody had expected her to appear like the ghost of Hamlet's father and derail her successor's plans, let alone try to reclaim her former position.

Really, it was typical of Grandma to refuse to stay put in the afterlife or let anyone take over from her. The bizarre urge to laugh hit me, and I pressed the back of my hand to my mouth.

Ramsey sat upright in his seat. "We have to restore order."

"Little late," I said. "I think that broom has taken flight."

The council members' arguing voices filled the aisle, while the woman who'd fainted was now quietly weeping in the corner. I peered at her, recognising her as Stacy, Grandma's former assistant. She wasn't the only person in tears, though other members of the crowd simply sat stunned in their seats and didn't move when Mum told them to leave. Loud objections broke out, and my headache returned with a vengeance.

"Enough!" Mum said loudly. "As your coven leader, I am ordering you to leave. Nobody is to contact the ghost of the former Head Witch without my permission."

I didn't see how she could possibly enforce that rule, but then again, Grandma was more likely to have relocated to our house than anywhere else.

Several witches raised their voices in protest, but Mum silenced them all with a look. "Go on. I'll let everyone know when I have an update on the Head Witch's situation."

For now, the sceptre would stay put. Grandma couldn't wield it, and it hadn't accepted or rejected anyone else yet, which left the position still open. I suspected Mum wouldn't try to redo the ceremony until Grandma's ghost was gone, but most spirits didn't typically stay in this world for long.

Why had she come back? Come to think of it, there was no better person to question about the Head Witch's murder than the woman herself... and if she *had* moved to our house, then I wouldn't be going against Mum's orders by talking to her.

Ramsey snagged my arm as I walked out of the hall. "Don't you even think about it."

I pulled the sleeve of my robe out of his grip. "I'm going home to change, assuming there isn't a ghost in my room. Unless you want to come and help me speak to her about whether or not she was murdered?"

Ramsey's eyes narrowed. "Absolutely not."

"Who better to ask than her ghost?" We'd yet to resolve yesterday's argument, but I was willing to let his accusations slide for the time being if he backed me up. "You're supposed to be the head of the law enforcement, so if she *was* murdered, then it's your job to arrest the killer."

He pinched the bridge of his nose. "Her being a ghost doesn't mean she was murdered. Becoming a spirit has more to do with the person's character, and Grandma was likely reluctant to move on."

"I bet she was, but she might have had unfinished business," I pressed. "That's common with spirits, isn't it?"

Ghosts definitely weren't my area of expertise. They weren't Ramsey's either, but he gave a firm shake of his head. "There's nothing she left unfinished that we can't handle ourselves, and it's better for everyone if she moved on."

As an ex-Head Witch, she was capable of causing the coven some serious headaches if she'd retained any of her former power, but even an atypical ghost like her wouldn't stick around forever. If we wanted answers about her death, I needed to find her.

9

Despite Mum's orders for everyone to leave the witches' headquarters, there were an awful lot of people in the grounds when Ramsey and I went outside. While nobody would have admitted to searching for the ghost of our former Head Witch, they'd gathered in groups to peer through windows or climb over hedges. When I saw several people enter the maze, I rolled my eyes. "If anyone else falls into the fountain, it'll be entirely their own fault."

Ramsey approached the maze and raised his voice. "Get out of there. The maze is still off-limits."

The group of witches ignored him, disappearing among the high hedges. Ramsey exhaled in a sigh then muttered something under his breath. A cloud of birds descended from the sky onto the maze, and a moment later, the witches emerged in a shrieking mass, batting the birds away from their heads. A grin came to my mouth. Ramsey rarely used his magic these days, preferring to wield the law instead, but sometimes the situation called for it.

"Want me to get Tansy to chase them off?" I asked him.

"No need," he said. "They weren't looking for our grandmother's ghost in there. I think they were trying to sneak a look around the fountain."

"You don't think *Tessa's* ghost might make an appearance?" I couldn't resist approaching the maze myself and peering through the hedges.

"No," Ramsey said. "She wasn't a very strong witch."

He walked towards the maze without telling me to leave, so I assumed we'd made a temporary truce. At least it gave me the chance to temporarily defrost the ice which had sprung up between us following his unfounded accusations. Speaking of which, he had yet to apologise for that, but until we found the person who'd actually blabbed to the press, I had no way to prove my innocence.

Besides, Grandma's ghost had brought a more pressing issue to deal with. She was nowhere to be found inside the maze and didn't appear to be anywhere else in the grounds, either.

"Might she have gone home?" I asked.

Ramsey began to head back towards the coven's headquarters. "Did she ever voluntarily leave work early in her life?"

"Fair point," I acknowledged. "Ghosts tend to stick to haunting one place, don't they? Though she *is* a former Head Witch, so she might be stronger than the average spirit."

"Strong or not, she thinks she's still Head Witch. She's more likely to have gone into her office than anywhere else."

We weren't the only people who'd had that thought, it seemed. Inside the coven's headquarters, we found a number of witches and wizards roaming the lobby. Grandma's office door was unlocked, as we discovered when Ramsey opened it to reveal Stacy crouching near the cabinet at the back.

Grandma's former assistant jumped when we entered, dropping an armful of herbs on the floor.

"Are you raiding Grandma's ingredient supplies?" Ramsey eyed the herbs in her arms. "What're those for?"

"I thought your mum might want to try summoning her ghost," she mumbled.

I gave the ingredients a closer look. "Sage repels ghosts. It doesn't summon them." Even I remembered that much.

Stacy flushed. "I didn't know—sorry."

She dropped the rest of the herbs on the floor and fled the room. Ramsey retrieved the ingredients, while I pushed the door shut so nobody else decided to sneak in.

"Bit slow, isn't she?" I remarked. "Why'd Grandma pick her as her assistant?"

"Felt sorry for her, I think." Ramsey closed the door on Grandma's ingredient supply cupboard. "She was failing her classes at the academy, so Grandma gave her some one-to-one lessons."

I raised a brow. "Wow, that makes me feel even better about her refusing to give me an apprenticeship."

"You didn't fail your exams."

I hadn't, but my marks had been average, which was as good as a failure in Mum's eyes. Nothing less than astounding would have sufficed. "If I had, then maybe she'd get off my case."

The office didn't contain any hiding places for a wandering ghost, and aside from the ingredients Stacy had dropped on the floor, none of the drawers and cabinets looked to have been disturbed recently.

Ramsey closed the cabinet door. "You could easily be as powerful a witch as Mum if you put your mind to it."

"It's not all about power, is it?" I had none of the other qualities required in a coven leader, and besides, Mum had held the title for less than a day. I didn't need to start thinking about who her successor might be. "If anything, that's the least important part of being coven leader. Or Head Witch."

Grandma had been a force to be reckoned with in her prime, but it was her skill at navigating the minefield of relations between covens as well as other paranormals which had won her the respect of the magical world at large. It didn't surprise me that her reappearance as an irrational ghost who might not even know she was dead had shaken everyone up.

Ramsey locked the office door once we'd left the room. "I'm going to look for Mum."

"I hope she locked her own office." Not that she'd be using it for much longer, since she'd relocate to Grandma's at the first opportunity. Assuming its former owner didn't object.

What a mess.

I returned to the back garden and spotted Tansy sitting on a nearby fence. "Found your ghost yet?"

"You heard?"

"The whole *town* heard," said Tansy. "Who would have thought your grandmother would come back from the dead?"

"Nobody did." I peered over the fence into the Henbane Coven's garden. If they'd been the ones who'd killed Grandma, I doubted they'd counted on her coming back from the dead. "I wonder if she's haunting anyone in particular."

"I'd say it's more likely that she's hiding," said Tansy.

"That's not her style." I paced along the fence, smelling the faint aroma of herbs that reminded me of Grandma's ingredient cabinet. "I wonder if using a summoning spell to find her would work."

"If it did, do you think she's any more likely to listen to you than she did earlier?"

Good point. Even if I managed to summon her ghost—and I'd never used that particular spell before—Grandma hadn't even been willing to listen to her own children, let alone me. "No, but as long as she's out there, we'll have a hard time picking another Head Witch."

Only Grandma could clear up the rumours about her death and leave a clear path ahead for the next Head Witch to be chosen so we could all get on with our lives. Yet no matter how long and hard we searched, she didn't reappear.

When it began to grow dark, Tansy yawned. "Everyone else has gone home, Robin. I think we should give up the search for now."

"And do what, wait for her to show up at the next ceremony?" That didn't seem much of a solution either.

"It won't take that long," she said. "You know she likes to be in charge. As soon as your mum starts taking on the coven's responsibilities, she'll show up again."

"Perhaps." Summoning her ghost was starting to look more and more appealing by the second. I finished my circuit of the garden and heard the distant murmur of voices from within the maze. "Who's in there? I thought Mum warded the place."

Tansy climbed my shoulder and dug in her claws. "Don't go back in there."

"Someone has to." I trod closer, listening. Wait. That was Mum's voice… and Aunt Shannon's.

"This is out of control," Mum was saying as I neared the maze's entrance. "The press has been spreading rumours that the Head Witch was murdered, and her ghost's reappearance isn't going to help the situation at all."

"What did you expect?" Aunt Shannon replied. "The only surprising part is that it took this long."

"For someone to tattle to the press?" Mum said. "So you aren't going to admit to anything?"

"The press doesn't need to interview any of us to come up with lies," she said. "They'll print anything that they think will sell, and this story practically writes itself. The coven leader's ghost returning is going to back up their rumours about the circumstances of her death without any of us needing to give them another word."

"The Head Witch will hardly support their rumours," Mum said. "She doesn't even know she's dead."

"The press don't know that, do they?" Aunt Shannon gave a soft laugh. "All they'll know is that she interrupted the ceremony and prevented you from claiming the sceptre. The Head Witch might not have remembered her fate, but her actions were clear enough. She doesn't think you're worthy of the title."

My mouth fell open. *She didn't just say that.*

"The Head Witch interrupted because she thinks she's

still alive," Mum said in calm tones. "Every single person in attendance witnessed the same scene as you and I did. The press can't rewrite a scene witnessed by hundreds of individuals."

"You and I know they can do whatever they like, Roxanne," Aunt Shannon said. "Look at the foul rumours they printed about our mother when she was alive… and look at how they correctly guessed that you were the last to speak to her before her death."

Having had enough, I rounded the corner and walked into view of the pair of them squaring up to one another beside the dragon-headed fountain. "I take it you didn't find her?"

"What are you doing in here?" Aunt Shannon asked.

"Same as everyone else, I assume," I said. "Looking for Grandma. You know her ghost can hide herself from human eyes, don't you? She might even be listening to you right now."

Aunt Shannon gave another of her fake laughs. "Mark my words, she'll be gone in a day, with or without our encouragement. I'd suggest you figure out how to deal with the aftermath."

She walked away while Mum watched her with a deceptively still expression. The tension in her posture reminded me of a predator about to pounce, and it took a great deal of self-control not to back away myself. "What's wrong with her? Is she that rattled over Grandma's ghost that she'd rather fling accusations at you than admit she did that interview herself? Or Vanessa. One of the two."

"She's not afraid of ghosts." Mum's voice was as dangerously bland as her expression. "She's angry that her scheming came to naught."

"Did she expect to be chosen as coven leader?" I'd assumed she'd known that Mum had pretty much been guaranteed the position from the moment she'd cast her first spell. "Or Head Witch?"

"I think part of her always held onto the hope of bucking the trend," she said. "She hoped the press's unsavoury rumours might discredit me."

"She gave them the story herself, didn't she?" I asked. "Ramsey accused *me* of doing the interview."

"I know," she said. "I set him right."

"You did?" Surprise leaked into my tone. "He... he blamed me because of that time I talked to the press when I was a kid."

"That was a long time ago." She gave me a considering look. "You did a good job at the ceremony. Maybe you should consider applying as Tessa's permanent replacement."

My mouth parted, my heart sinking. Every compliment she gave was a double-edged sword, a reminder of my supposed natural role as her successor. "I did tell you I already have a job, right? Also, someone murdered her."

"Not for that reason." Mum's tone held enough certainty that I found myself wondering if she knew more than she'd let on about Tessa's death after all. "She didn't have a prominent role in the coven."

"Grandma did." It wasn't a good idea to prod her when she was in such a variable mood, but how many more chances would we have to speak to her mother about her death? "Have you considered talking to her?"

Her gaze sharpened. "Don't start, Robin."

So much for not arguing with her. "Grandma's ghost

might be avoiding us, but she's still here. She can answer questions."

"She's not avoiding us, she's lost and confused," said Mum. "Most likely, she's waiting for everyone to leave so she can try to claim the sceptre again. She's in no condition to answer any questions."

"But—"

"Last I heard, I was coven leader, not you, Robin," she said. "*I* will handle my mother and see to it that she departs before I become Head Witch."

It was a testament to her self-confidence that she still harboured no obvious doubts that she'd be chosen for the position, but I was less than convinced. What if Grandma did end up sticking around long term, like some ghosts did? She was bound to remember her death eventually if she did, but the amount of trouble she might cause in the process might not be worth the trade-off. Still, I knew a dismissal when I heard one, so I left the maze.

When I rejoined Tansy, a tarantula-shaped shadow stretched across my path, and I jumped when its owner emerged from the gazebo. "Rowan, don't scare me like that."

"Sorry, Robin." She crouched to let her familiar climb onto her hand. "I didn't know anyone else was still around."

Hadn't she heard Mum and Aunt Shannon arguing? "Are you looking for Grandma too?"

"Nope," she said. "You know her. She'll show up again when she feels like it."

I had to admit she was probably right, given that nobody had managed to find her yet. "She had to make a public display, didn't she?"

"The surprising part to me is that everyone else *was* surprised," said Rowan. "Don't get me wrong, it freaked me out as well, but it makes sense for her to come back. She never officially named a successor."

"You think she had unfinished business?" I asked. "She doesn't get to choose the next Head Witch whether she's dead or alive, though. That's up to the sceptre."

"She wouldn't let a little thing like death stop her, would she?" Rowan said. "She never wanted to retire."

"A ghost can't run a coven, let alone act as Head Witch," I reminded her. "Surely everyone who saw her public display would admit that she clearly wasn't chosen by the sceptre. She couldn't even *touch* it."

"No, but they aren't going to take its actions as an endorsement of your mother, either, are they?" Rowan asked. "It didn't choose anyone."

"I know," I said. "Grandma can't take the position, though. Her ghost won't be around forever."

"No," she said. "Won't stop the press printing their rumours, though."

"I guess you saw." Everyone had probably read that article by now, but did she realise her mother and sister had likely been responsible? "Nice of them to make everyone think Grandma was murdered."

She gave the slightest flinch. "You don't think that… do you?"

I'd assumed the thought had at least crossed her mind after Vanessa's taunts yesterday, but perhaps she'd seen her sister as simply trying to wind me up. "I think the press will tell any lie to get a good story. They're unscrupulous. I can't believe Ramsey accused *me* of tattling to them."

"He did what?" Her eyes widened, while Ralph hid himself behind her hair. "That's not cool at all."

"I know, right?" I shook my head. "He still hasn't apologised, but he must know I wouldn't tell tales on our family, especially at a time like this."

Her mouth pressed together. "I should head home before my mum comes looking for me."

"I thought you might have seen her leaving the maze." Come to think of it, I hadn't seen Mum leave either. Which meant she'd removed the wards on the back entrance, or she was still there, listening to us. "She was arguing with my mum."

She winced. "I bet she's mad after losing out on the coven leadership title."

"And the ghost incident." I didn't envy her for having to go home to that, though being around Mum and Ramsey was hardly appealing either.

Regardless, I'd been here almost all day, and I was starving, so I left the coven's headquarters with Rowan, and we parted ways outside our respective houses. As I entered the hallway, my foot landed on something half fluffy, half spiky, which yowled loudly and stuck its claws in my leg.

"Ow!" I hopped on the spot. "Carmilla… wait, have *you* seen Grandma?"

Carmilla gave a baleful meow and walked out of the hall, while I rubbed my sore leg, wondering if she even knew her owner had come back as a ghost. If not, she'd want me to tell her, right?

"Carmilla." I followed her into the living room. "Grandma's ghost appeared at the ceremony and tried to pick up the sceptre."

The cat laid down on the carpet next to Mum's sleeping familiar, displaying nothing but indifference to my words. She might have decided to stop communicating with any of us after Grandma's death, but there was nothing wrong with her hearing as far as I was aware. Why was she ignoring me?

I jumped when my phone buzzed in my pocket. Pulling it out, I found a text from a number I didn't know. *Hope you're okay. Want to meet up at the Fox's Den later so you can tell me about it all? - Harvey.*

Harvey. Since when had I given him my number? Last night, I assumed, though my memories were a little fuzzy. I couldn't have done anything too heinous if he wanted to see me again, and for a moment, I was tempted to take him up on his offer. On the other hand, I still had a lingering headache from last night, and besides, wandering around in the dark didn't strike me as a good idea.

I typed a reply. *Can I check back with you tomorrow? Bit tired.*

Ramsey entered the living room. "Thought I heard you come in."

I sent the message and indicated the fluffy black cat. "Reckon she knows her witch is back?"

"No." He crouched down to stroke her, and she nipped at his hand, so he sank into an armchair, and Prickles crawled onto his lap instead. "I should probably assign some security to the coven's headquarters overnight in case anyone tries to go ghost hunting."

"Don't go yourself," I said. "You'll fall asleep within two minutes."

His eyelids were already drooping. "I'm not tired."

"Sure you aren't." I headed towards the kitchen. "I'm going to make hot chocolate and have an early night. Want some?"

He stifled a yawn. "I'm not sure I'd trust you to make a glass of water, to be honest."

"How very dare you." I shot him a grin, glad that he seemed to have put our argument aside. "I can order takeout and put a film on. How does that sound?"

Ramsey frowned at me, but he took my offered truce. "I need to assign someone to watch the coven's headquarters first."

"Can the others on your team even *see* ghosts?" Even witches and wizards didn't always have the gift, though everyone in my family did. I could only imagine how weird the ceremony had looked to the attendees who'd only been able to see the floating sceptre without any of Grandma's antics. "Hey, maybe we can lure her back to the house if we put on one of her favourite movies. Something with lots of explosions."

"You think that'll work?" His words dripped with scepticism.

"It's no less likely than her showing up at the coven's headquarters while everyone is flocking around like a swarm of pigeons."

10

My plan to summon Grandma back via a movie night was a dismal failure, but my brother and I managed to get through the night without another argument. Mostly because we both fell asleep in the middle of the film. I woke up for long enough to drag myself to bed and crash again and then awoke late in the morning to a barrage of text messages.

From the constant ringing sound from downstairs, I guessed people were calling the house, too, perhaps to ask Mum if she'd found the ghost or if she'd decided when to reschedule the ceremony for the new Head Witch to be chosen. She ought to have set a temporary deadline to get them off her back for five minutes, but I didn't blame her for not having a contingency plan for the sudden appearance of the ghost of the former Head Witch.

After a quick shower, I dressed and went downstairs, the phone's incessant ringing filling the background. Ramsey was presumably back at work, while Mum wasn't around either. I guessed she'd gone to the coven's headquarters, either in search of Grandma's ghost or to stop anyone else from swarming the place. While I'd have liked to grab a latte from Were's My Coffee?, I didn't need to make it easier for the press to ambush me.

Before I could begin to figure out the coffee maker, my phone began to ring, so I took the call.

"Hey, Dad. I guess you heard?"

"I did," he said. "Want to come and talk in person? Or does your mother have you confined to the house?"

"Not officially." She wouldn't be thrilled if she came back and found me gone, but staying at home and waiting for Grandma's ghost to show up again didn't appeal to me in the slightest. Besides, I knew a route to Dad's house via the woodland paths which the press ought to be unaware of. "I can come over, but only if there aren't any reporters around."

"There aren't," he said. "They haven't found our house yet. Also, I have coffee."

"Well, *now* I'm coming." I grinned. "I figured it's not worth the risk of running into the press for the sake of getting a latte."

"If you leave now, you can join us for breakfast."

"I'll be on my way." Ignoring the still-ringing phone, I went looking for Tansy and found her raiding the bird feeders in the back garden again. When I beckoned to her, she came scurrying over. "You're heading out?"

"I'm going to my dad's," I said. "Want to come? I bet the kids will love you."

"I *am* loveable," Tansy agreed. She scurried alongside me as I made my way to the gate leading into the woods.

The faint sound of birdsong in the background masked the ringing in my ears from that wretched phone and reminded me of the boost to my magic from being back in my coven's territory. I stuck to a lesser-known route out of coven territory and towards the werewolves' area of town to avoid running into anyone. This far out, I was more at risk of encountering a nude werewolf than any reporters, since the wolves and other shifters typically lived close to the forest to avoid making a public spectacle when they shifted back and forth between their human and animal forms.

Jessica owned a nice cottage in a grove surrounded by oak trees, with plenty of space for her twin werewolf sons to run around to their hearts' content. Dad had dealt with no end of mockery from certain members of the coven when he'd moved out of Mum's house to what they described as a shack in the woods, but I found the cottage much more pleasant.

Jessica answered the door when I knocked. Blond like most werewolves, she had a friendly face and wore a pair of leggings patterned with squirrels.

"I like her already," Tansy said, scurrying up my arm to perch on my shoulder.

"Hey," I said to Jessica. "Did Dad tell you I was coming?"

"He did, but you're always welcome to drop in and visit." She backed into the hallway. "I have to drop the boys off at school in half an hour, but they'll be excited to meet you again."

Her twin sons from her previous marriage, Jake and Spike, would be around six or seven now. I hadn't seen them since they were toddlers, so there was a good chance they wouldn't remember me. Two blond kids sat building some kind of Lego construction in the living room, and

Dad beamed at me when I came in. "Jake, Spike, do you remember Robin?"

"No," said one of the boys. "Is that a squirrel?"

"This is Tansy." I showed them my familiar, who put on a show of climbing over my back and waving her bushy tail for their entertainment. They were soon enthralled, and once they'd figured out who I was, they were all too keen to show off their Lego collection and watch Tansy's antics. Jessica had to coax them to get their coats on and get ready for school and waved to Dad and me before ushering them out the door.

Dad watched them leave, a smile on his face. "They grow up so fast. They're doing great at school sports too."

"Bet they're adorable when they shift," I said.

He went into the kitchen and set two mugs of coffee on the table. "They are, but they leave so much fur everywhere, I have to vacuum three times a day."

"Keeps life interesting, right?"

I followed him into the kitchen and helped myself to the promised coffee and toast. For a short while, I'd almost forgotten the coven and Grandma's ghost, but Dad would expect an update, and frankly, I didn't even know where to start. I sipped my coffee instead, while Tansy explored the house. Dad didn't seem to mind her scurrying around, but a squirrel wasn't any worse than a couple of excitable werewolf kids.

I was glad Dad had Jake and Spike to keep him company, considering Ramsey had mostly stopped keeping in contact after he and Mum had divorced. The coven had taken Mum's side, too, and Mum herself hadn't helped matters by insisting that Ramsey and I put the coven first.

Dad broke the silence first. "I know it's probably rough at your mother's house, but I'm guessing you'd rather stay there than sleep on the sofa here for the next couple of nights. Jessica wouldn't mind if you did."

I was pretty sure Mum would rather I camped in the garden. "It's not too bad, but I think Mum's at the coven's headquarters. The phone's been ringing all day, since she's gone and Ramsey's at work. How'd you find out?"

"Jessica said another werewolf told her," he said.

"That was fast," I said. "I thought Mum might have told you…"

"You know she never tells me anything."

"You and me both," I murmured. "What did the rumour mill say, then?"

"The former Head Witch's ghost showed up and stopped your mother from claiming the sceptre."

"She thought she was still alive," I clarified. "Grandma's ghost did, I mean. She appeared and tried to pick up the sceptre herself. When it didn't work, she disappeared and left everyone in a panic."

"I bet," he said. "Do you know what caused her to come back?"

"I think she came back of her own accord," I said. "I mean, it's possible she was summoned by someone, but given her behaviour, it's more likely she did it herself."

"It seems in character for the Head Witch to return from death," he said. "She was dedicated to her job."

"To the extent that she worked right up until she died." I took a long sip of coffee, debating how much to tell him. "Ghosts often come back because of unfinished business, don't they?"

"Yes, they do."

Tansy ran up to sit on the table, her tail sticking up in the air. "Especially when—"

I shot her a warning look, which silenced her. Dad cleared his throat. "Especially when… what?"

I didn't want to drag Dad further into this mess, but it wasn't as if he was likely to know any more than I did about the possibility of the Head Witch's death not being accidental. "There's a chance that the Head Witch didn't die of natural causes."

His eyes widened. "Does your brother think so?"

"I think he suspects, but he's trying to keep it quiet. You know how he is."

Sadness flickered in his eyes. "Yes, I do."

I wished I hadn't brought him up, but it was hard not to mention my brother when it came to matters which concerned the police. "We're not certain, though, but it'd help if we could track down her ghost. Since she doesn't know she's dead and wants the sceptre back, everyone thinks she's undermining Mum's authority."

"I bet your mother's unhappy," said Dad. "She always did like to be in control."

"A trait she got from *her* mother," I added. "Also, if you have any tips for attracting a ghost, I'm all ears."

"Ghosts want attention," he said. "Not that I'm an expert, but we had a ghost show up in a house we were renovating once, and all he wanted was to be noticed. Your grandmother… I doubt she'll stay hidden for long. It's not in her nature."

I turned this over in my mind. "Okay. I hope Mum has the same idea, because she doesn't seem inclined to listen to me at the moment."

He grimaced. "Your mother's under pressure. Do try not to take anything she says to heart."

"I'm trying not to." The accusations of blabbing to the press had stung, but they'd mostly come from Ramsey, who was under enough pressure of his own this week. Besides, Mum of all people had set him right on that one, and we'd had a companionable movie night yesterday, even if I'd slept through most of it. "It doesn't help that I'm pretty sure she agrees that Grandma's death wasn't an accident, but she refuses to acknowledge it aloud."

"She's certainly stubborn," he said. "And concerned for you, I'd wager."

"Yeah." I put down my empty mug. "The problem is, there's a chance Tessa was murdered too. Maybe by the same person. I think Mum knows, but she doesn't want word to spread around the rest of the coven. She's already dealing with their demands, and… well, you've probably seen what the *Blue Moon* said."

"I make a point of ignoring anything they publish," he said.

"Good idea." They'd printed some pretty nasty stuff about him and my mother when they'd been in the process of getting their divorce. Not that the press had had anything nice to say when they'd been together either, since they'd gained a lot of business from spreading rumours about the future Head Witch marrying below her station. That above all had taught me that there was no pleasing them. "The problem is, someone close to the family did an interview with the *Blue Moon* this week and told them about Grandma's death not being accidental. We still haven't found out who, but it definitely wasn't me."

He muttered a curse under his breath. "Awful people. They've been outside our house, too, but Jessica shifted and howled a little to make them go away. She let the boys get in on it too."

I burst out laughing. "That's brilliant. They haven't come to pester you since?"

"No, they had the sense to stay away after that," he said. "I hope they didn't hassle you too much."

"I didn't say a word to them, but someone did, and they can spin a false story out of a single sentence if they want to."

The coven might have been their current focus, but I'd seen them go after anyone from regular folk to minor celebrities with an equal level of biting criticism and cruel jabs. How could Ramsey think I'd ever go and give them the dirt on our family, even if I'd had reason to be mad at Mum and him?

"Don't pay them any attention." He checked the time on his phone. "I'd better get ready. I have a job on the other side of town in an hour."

I went to the sink to wash my dirty mug and plate. "Thanks for inviting me over."

"You're always welcome here," he said. "You know that, right? Jessica agrees, and the boys would be thrilled to have you around too."

I blinked, my eyes stinging unexpectedly. "Thanks. It means a lot to hear that after the week I've had."

"I bet." He pulled me into a hug from behind. "Don't let them get you down."

"I won't." I finished washing up and beckoned to Tansy to follow me.

After we left my dad's house, we returned to the

woodland path and began to walk home. The soothing hum of the Wildwood's magic filled the background, and I kept my pace slow to delay the inevitable moment I had to face my family again. Upon reaching the back entrance to Mum's house, I stilled at the sound of voices coming from somewhere nearby, not on the ground but in the air.

I lifted my head to see a flock of broomsticks above the forest, high enough that I recognised their formation. They were playing Sky Hopper. Not kids but professionals judging by their bright-red uniforms. Was Harvey among them? I stood on tiptoe, tilting my head back to see if I could spot him, but they were too high up, moving so fast they blurred before my eyes.

"Wow."

"No thanks," Tansy said in my ear. "That's too high up even for me."

"Same here, but it's entertaining to watch."

Sky Hopper had a complicated series of rules which revolved around each team levitating hoops around in mid-air without the opposing team stealing their hoops first. I'd never been much use on a broomstick, but I did enjoy watching their manoeuvres as they attempted to undercut one another. I was so fixated on the sky that I didn't notice I had company until Tansy hissed and brought my attention to ground level—where I found myself nose to nose with Leona, Tiffany Henbane's assistant. "What're you doing here?"

Why was she lurking behind my mother's house? Had she been hoping to snag some gossip on the situation with the Head Witch's ghost? Up close, she looked even younger than she had at the funeral, maybe seventeen at most.

"I was on a walk to gather some herbs, and I got distracted by them." She pointed up at the formation of broomsticks. "Hard to miss. They're very good, aren't they?"

"Yeah." They were too. Wildwood Heath's team was the best in the region, though until now, I hadn't been personally acquainted with anyone who played. I had to admit my interest had climbed after I'd learned about Harvey's involvement, and I wondered if his offer to meet him at the Fox's Den was still open. If I dared to leave the coven's territory and risk running into the press, of course. He didn't deserve their mockery any more than poor Dad did. No, I'd have to be patient and wait until all this died down.

Or not, because I wasn't supposed to be staying in town, no matter how good he might be at flying.

Leona gave me a curious look. "I'm surprised you're walking around outside, considering… you know."

My shoulders tensed. "Considering what? The ghost? She's not here."

"The fact that the old Head Witch showed up to cast doubt on her successor, of course."

Not this again. "That's not why she showed up. Who told you that?"

"Everyone's talking about it," she said. "She stopped the ceremony, didn't she?"

"She thought she was still alive," I corrected. "She was a typical ghost, wandering around with no idea she was dead, and she tried to pick up the sceptre because she thought it should still belong to her. She wasn't trying to undermine Mum. She barely knew she was there."

"That's not what I heard, but I suppose you were there in person and I wasn't," she said.

"That's right." I didn't particularly want to chat to her, but maybe now was as good a time as any to ask her a couple of questions. She was certainly more present than Grandma's ghost at the moment, anyway. "Where'd you hear about it?"

"Tiffany heard from another witch," she replied. "She also said you took Tessa's job."

"Temporarily," I clarified. "Since they needed someone to step in at the last minute."

"Of course," she said. "I suppose you're the next in line now, though."

Annoyance flared. "That's the coven's business, not yours."

"Did I overstep? I apologise." Her tone didn't suggest she was very sorry at all. "I expect your mother will want to wrap everything up fast, even with a ghost on the loose."

"You mean the Head Witch ceremony?" Not that *that* was any of her business either. "I wouldn't know."

"I only thought…" She trailed off. "I mean, I guess nobody has ever seen a Head Witch make an appearance from beyond the grave before."

"Don't get too excited," I said. "She's not taking visitors."

I opened the gate and headed back to the house, already wondering if I'd been rude to her for no good reason, but her excuse for lurking around behind our fence sounded like a blatant lie. Gathering herbs, was she? Admittedly, clumps of nettles and similar plants abounded in the woods behind the garden, but she could have picked any similar spot in the Wildwood which wasn't anywhere near my mother's house.

Once I was on the other side of the gate, I turned to Tansy. "Want to follow her and see if she's up to any mischief?"

"Way ahead of you."

While she scurried over the fence, I walked through the garden to the house, narrowly avoiding tripping over Carmilla on the way in. The cat hissed at me when I crouched down beside her.

"Going to answer my questions today?" I asked.

Carmilla yawned in my face, while I straightened upright with a rush of determined resolve.

If we didn't want to wait around all week to see what other horror stories the press constructed, I'd have to convince the rest of my family that summoning and questioning Grandma's ghost was the only way to find answers. And if I couldn't? I'd do it alone.

11

I went searching for Mum, but when I heard her voice drifting out of the kitchen, I found myself walking on tiptoe as if I was a kid again.

"No, we aren't going to reschedule yet," she was saying to someone on the phone. "Do you want another interruption from a ghost? Try to have some patience. Call me tomorrow."

I entered the kitchen as she ended the call, and her attention snapped onto me. "Where have you been?"

"To see Dad and Jessica." I knew that would annoy her, but it was one of the few reasons I might get away without a lecture. It was usually hard to tell what her reaction would be to me bringing up Dad, though, since she rarely mentioned him—which suited Ramsey just fine. Me, not so much.

"Did you now." Her tone was neutral, but her eyebrow twitch gave away her disapproval. She never had liked Jessica, and while she hadn't remarried after her split with Dad, she hadn't wanted to. To be perfectly honest, I wasn't entirely sure she'd loved Dad. She had adhered firmly to the coven's expectations that she marry and have kids who'd be the next potential coven leaders, the same as Grandma had.

"I ran into Leona around the back of our garden, by the way," I added. "From the Henbane Coven. I think she was trying to get a look in to see if Grandma's ghost showed up."

"And what did she have to say for herself?"

"Not much, except she implied she believes the nonsense the press said about the ghost showing up to undermine your authority."

A scowl appeared on her mouth. "Typical."

"Have you seen Grandma's ghost?" I asked. "Since yesterday, I mean?"

"No," she said sharply. "Not that I've had a moment's peace all day. The rest of the coven seems to think that constantly hounding me is the best way to bring her back."

"I'm not sure we can bet on her disappearing quietly without a fuss," I said carefully. "And if you don't want to delay the Head Witch ceremony any longer, maybe we should take matters into our own hands."

She narrowed her eyes. "In what way?"

"Summoning her ghost ourselves," I said. "Then we can convince her to cede the position of Head Witch to you."

"As if she'd listen," Mum said. "She refuses to believe she's dead, and I doubt even I can persuade her otherwise."

"Maybe she'd be willing to listen if we aren't in front of a few hundred witnesses," I said. "If it doesn't work, nobody will know. A summoning spell is relatively simple, right?"

"I'm perfectly aware of how to conduct a ghost-summoning spell," Mum said. "Though the ethics of summoning a potentially dangerous spirit comes close to breaking some of our laws."

"It's not against the law if there's no other way to be rid of her, right?" I asked. "I mean, you could ask a Reaper to help, but they'd leave us with no chance to question her beforehand."

"Who said anything about questioning her?"

I searched her face. "Don't you want to know for sure if her death was natural or not?"

"I think she's in no position to tell us anything." Her expression remained unreadable. "And summoning her ourselves is more likely to agitate her."

"Isn't that better than her interrupting another ceremony and wreaking havoc again?" I pressed. "If we summoned her, we'd be in total control, within reason. We can do it at the coven's headquarters if you'd rather she didn't end up haunting our house, unless it's still full of coven members hoping to find her ghost."

"I sealed the entire building to prevent anyone from entering until her ghost is found," she said. "I also sealed the supply cupboards in case anyone gets any ideas."

"So nobody else can summon her," I guessed. "Wait. Leona was gathering herbs in the woods. I wonder if *she* was attempting to throw together a summoning spell."

If she was, I hoped Tansy would catch her in the act. A spell for summoning a ghost had several common herbs and plants, including nettles and thyme, both of which grew in the woods. You'd think the Henbane Coven would have their own supplies, though.

Mum's mouth pulled down at the corners. "My mother wouldn't appear to her and not us."

"So you agree, then?" My gaze landed on Carmilla, who'd wandered into the room behind us. "Have you got a word out of Carmilla since Grandma's ghost came back?"

Mum looked at the cat as though she'd forgotten she existed. "No, she's refusing to speak, and I'm not sure she can hear well either. She's very old for a cat."

"She's alert enough to keep trying to trip me up in doorways." I frowned when Mum conjured up her cloak and headed for the front door. "Wait, are you going to the coven's headquarters?"

"What do you think?" She didn't slow, barely allowing me the chance to catch her up before heading outside and towards the large shape of the coven's base.

Shimmering wards covered the front of the building like a semitransparent forcefield from a sci-fi movie, but Mum undid them with a wave of her wand.

She's serious. She'd actually gone along with my idea. Maybe she wanted the ghost gone badly enough to put aside our disagreements, but I wouldn't complain either way.

After Mum unlocked the coven's storeroom, I went to collect the right herbs for a summoning spell. Nettles, thyme, and a ground mixture of herbs in a container which may or may not have contained actual grave dust. I didn't remember the details.

I retreated from the room with my arms laden with the ingredients. "Want to do the summoning in an empty classroom?"

"Any will do." Mum pushed open the door to the nearest room and turned on the light. Rows of wooden desks and plastic chairs faced the front, while Mum waved her wand to move some of them aside to clear a space on the floor. I, meanwhile, started to lay out the herbs according to my memories of my academy lessons. I'd always been better at practical spells than anything written, but it wasn't long before Mum's need to be in control came out.

"Put them in a circle," she said. "No gaps. And try not to tread on anything."

I sheepishly moved away from the piles of leaves which were inches from my foot. "Should one of us stand near the door in case she tries to escape?"

"She's a ghost, Robin. You can't stop her from moving, and she can travel through the walls besides."

Right. Of course. I finished setting up the circle, my magic reacting to the anticipation by bringing a green glow to my palms. "Do you have the sceptre?"

"It's still in her office." Her mouth compressed. "I'll go and get it."

The merest hint of anger in her voice hinted at her true feelings about being thwarted in her quest to become Head Witch.

"Why not try without it first?" I suggested. "Grandma can't be far away. We'll find out pretty quickly if she's here."

"Fine." Mum faced the circle of herbs on the ground and said in a clear voice, "I wish to speak to Willow Wildwood."

A breeze stirred the leaves in the circle, and without a sound, Grandma's ghost appeared on the spot as if she'd been waiting there all along. I startled, not prepared for her to show up the instant we cast the spell. *Maybe we should have rehearsed this first.*

Grandma's transparent eyes travelled across me then fixated on Mum. "Where is my sceptre?"

"It's not yours any longer, Mother," said Mum. "You're not Head Witch. You're dead."

Grandma put on a scowl which mirrored her daughter's. "I'm still here, aren't I?"

I shook my head. "You aren't supposed to be here, Grandma."

"Neither are you," she said. "You left town."

"I came back for your funeral." Typical that she'd remind me of my failings even as a ghost. "And for the ceremony to name your successor. Then Tessa was murdered. Do you remember her?"

"Ah, Tessa," she said. "Always trying to get under my feet, she is."

"Is she?" At least she remembered who she was. "When did you last see her?"

"Oh, she was hanging around outside my office after I finished work for the day," she said. "I remember."

"Which day?" I pressed. "You mean the day you died?"

A moment of silence passed while Grandma looked askance at the pair of us. "Do neither of you have any respect for your Head Witch? I taught you better than that, Roxanne."

"You're dead, Mother," Mum said through gritted teeth. "You're no longer Head Witch. Do you remember your death at all?"

"Unbelievable." Grandma circled the room, her feet hovering above the ground. She *did* know she was dead.

"How like you, Roxanne, to sweep my life and accomplishments under the carpet."

"You told me to take over the coven in your place, Mother," said Mum. "You trained me for the job."

"I'm still here!" Her voice brought a sweeping gust of wind which knocked several chairs and tables over, while I fought the impulse to back away. "I won't be silenced."

"We want to listen to you." I attempted a placating tone. "Tessa was murdered, and the timing of your death was suspicious too. Who might have wanted you dead?"

"Oh, dozens of people." Grandma looked into my eyes, her expression startlingly alert for a ghost. "I'd appreciate it if you stopped ordering me around. I'm your Head Witch."

"You're dead," Mum repeated. "You won't be around forever."

"Says who?" She flew right out of the circle of herbs and made straight for the door. "I can stay as long as I like."

"Mother!" Mum shouted. "Get back here right now."

If she'd used that tone on anyone else, it might have worked, but the former Head Witch paid no attention. I could have sworn every door and window in the entire building rattled when she flew out of the room and into the lobby. A series of thuds followed, like books falling off shelves and furniture shifting around. Just what we needed… she'd gone full poltergeist.

Mum and I stared at each other for a moment, then she grabbed her wand. "Stay in here."

"Why not try to summon her back?" That wouldn't do much good if we couldn't keep her contained, though.

Why had I assumed the former Head Witch would listen to a word either of us said?

Mum ran out of the room and up the staircase, while the sound of Grandma's loud cackling echoed from above. A moment later, Mum came running back downstairs, her expression furious. "She's gone. Vanished into thin air again."

"I bet she's biding her time before she comes back." So much for an easy solution by summoning her ghost. "I should have known she wouldn't listen."

"You should have let me do the talking," Mum said.

You weren't doing any better than I was. "She wouldn't listen to either of us. You know that."

Yet she'd dropped one hint. What had she said about Tessa getting under her feet? Had Tessa been close enough that she'd known who'd been responsible for her death? Grandma hadn't seemed to know who her murderer had been, but if she'd died while asleep, it made sense that she'd been oblivious.

The front doors to the building flew open, and Aunt Shannon and Vanessa entered the lobby.

"I knew you'd come back at the first opportunity," Aunt Shannon spat at Mum. "You lied to me when you said you weren't going to attempt a summoning."

"I never said that," Mum said. "I said I wouldn't banish her ghost, and I decided it was worth trying to see if we could get answers from her."

"Also, it was my idea," I added. "There's nothing we can do to reschedule the Head Witch ceremony until her ghost is gone."

"If you didn't banish her, where did she go?" asked Vanessa.

"She disappeared, perhaps because *you* showed up," Mum said. "Until we find the person responsible for her death, however, then I would prefer for her to stay."

It was the first time she'd acknowledged it aloud. Vanessa's eyes grew as wide as dishes, but Aunt Shannon simply laughed.

"What?" I studied her. "I don't think her death was an accident either. Nobody does, thanks to that article."

"And who was to blame for that?" Vanessa glared at me.

"I didn't say a word to the reporters," I said. "But someone did."

I looked between the two of them, then at Mum, whose expression was stony. Apparently, nobody was inclined to confess to anything, but all eyes went to the front doors when they opened again and Ramsey walked in. "What is going on in here?"

"We summoned Grandma's ghost," I said before the others could start spinning their own stories.

"You mean *you* summoned her ghost?" he asked.

"No, Mum agreed to it," I said. "Unfortunately, it didn't quite go as planned."

Ramsey's expression turned to alarm. "Has she turned into a poltergeist?"

"Before she disappeared again, yes," I said.

"Then we'll find her." He headed for the stairs at once, calling out, "Grandma?"

"She's a ghost, not a cat," I reminded him. "Also, she still thinks she's in charge and won't listen to anyone else."

Ramsey climbed the stairs, followed by Mum. Aunt Shannon, meanwhile, waylaid me before I could leave the lobby. "I can hardly believe you talked your mother into summoning the Head Witch's ghost."

"As if you didn't plan to do the same yourself," I retaliated. "You came here for the same purpose. Don't try to deny it."

"I suppose you're trying to make up for the mishap earlier this week when you told tales on our family to the press."

"I didn't tell the bloody press a thing," I said.

"Nobody has forgotten that interview you did a few years ago, Robin," she said.

"Everyone makes mistakes."

"Like setting the ghost of the Head Witch loose?" said Vanessa.

"She was already here," I pointed out. "And if you don't mind, I'm going to find her."

I doubted she'd show up with half the family here, and besides, I'd learned my lesson from yesterday about hunting for Grandma when she clearly had no intention of being found. She wasn't in denial about being dead either. She just didn't care.

Tansy ran up to me as I exited the building, her tail bobbing with excitement. "You're not going to believe what I found."

12

I blinked at Tansy, then I remembered when I'd last seen her. "The Henbane Coven? You followed Leona, and… wait, she didn't try to get into the garden, did she?"

"No, but I found an interesting arrangement of herbs when I peeked through the window," she said. "It looked rather like a spell for summoning…"

"A ghost?" I headed through the gate which led into the back garden in order to avoid walking past Aunt Shannon or Vanessa again. "Is that why she vanished?"

"Who vanished?" Tansy scampered alongside me atop the fence as I closed the gate behind me. "Your grand-mother's ghost?"

"We summoned her," I explained. "Mum and I did."

"Your mother agreed to do that?"

"Believe me, she has regrets," I said. "And so do I. Where's this summoning spell?"

"This way." She ran ahead of me, across the top of the fence, while I did my best to ignore the raised voices drifting out of the lobby. It didn't surprise me that Aunt Shannon was irked at Mum for summoning Grandma's ghost after implying she had no intention of doing so, but I highly doubted the thought hadn't crossed her mind if even Tiffany had tried a summoning spell.

On the other hand, nothing Aunt Shannon or Vanessa had said had suggested that either of them was responsible for Grandma's death. The Henbane Coven, though… what possible reason might they have to cast a summoning spell if not to contact Grandma's ghost and get rid of it before she revealed the truth about her death?

While Tansy easily climbed over the fence, I had to return to the maze to find a route into the neighbouring garden. My attempt to climb over the hedge earned me scratches all over my legs, but I scrambled over and landed awkwardly on the lawn.

Tansy ran across the grass and then halted behind the Henbane Coven's headquarters, her tail sticking straight up in the air. "Look in there."

I peered through the window. I could see a circle of leaves and scatterings of herbs on a desk inside the room, but from this angle, I wasn't certain it resembled a ghost summoning spell. I needed to look closer to know for sure. The door to the room moved an inch or so.

"There's someone coming in!" Tansy hissed.

In a wild sprint of panic, I ran across the lawn and back to the spot where I'd climbed over. The slight problem? There were no hedges for me to climb over on this side.

I drew back and did a flying leap at the fence, which looked easier in the movies than it was in real life. My first attempt failed utterly. On my second, I leapt for the lowest-hanging branch of the oak tree on the other side of the fence and somehow grabbed it tightly enough to hang awkwardly in mid-air. From there, I managed a rare feat of upper body strength and pulled myself over the fence, crash-landing in the hedges on the other side.

I lay sprawled in a nest of leaves and branches as Tansy sprang down to join me. "I hope she didn't see me."

"She didn't," said Tansy. "But I reckon she's about to cover up the evidence of that spell if she hasn't already."

"Figures." I disentangled myself from the hedge and landed on the path.

A sudden loud creaking noise came from somewhere overhead.

"Move!" Tansy yelped. "Get out of there!"

She didn't need to tell me twice. I sprinted forwards, and an instant later, a huge tree branch slammed down, landing on the hedge in the same spot where I'd been lying. Twigs and leaves flew everywhere as the ground reverberated from the impact, and I legged it out of the maze into the main part of the garden before stopping to breathe.

"Whoa." My heart thumped in my chest. "That was a close one."

"That was deliberate," said Tansy tremulously. "Someone knocked that branch off on purpose. Look at it."

Breathless, I rotated on my heel. The huge branch had crushed an entire section of the hedge, but the rest of the giant oak tree looked as sturdy as ever. How could the branch have snapped off of its own accord? Either I'd knocked it off somehow when I'd jumped over the fence, or someone had tried to bring it down on my head.

Someone like one of the Henbane witches.

Movement out of the corner of my eye made me spin around, seeing Rowan hovering near the gazebo. "Oh, hey, Robin. What're you doing?"

"Nearly getting crushed by a fallen branch, apparently." I approached her, my heartbeat still unsteady. "Were you looking for the ghost?"

"No," she said. "I was looking for you."

"Why?" I asked. "Do you know your sister and mother are at the coven's headquarters?"

"Yes, which is why I'm here and not over there." She indicated the large building across the lawn. "What fallen branch?"

I headed back into the maze, while Tansy ran in panicked circles. "Don't go back in!"

"I have to find whoever knocked that branch down." Someone had tried to kill me.

Ignoring Tansy's noise of alarm, I ran straight up to the fence bordering the Henbane Coven's garden, and half-pulled myself up so I could see over the top. Splinters dug into my hands, but it was worth the sharp pain to see Leona jump violently. *I knew it was her.*

"Robin?" She peered up at me. "Did you let your familiar loose in my garden?"

"I didn't let my familiar loose anywhere." I remained hanging there, gripping the top of the fence for balance. "Someone just knocked a branch on top of me and nearly killed me."

"What?" Her eyes widened, but her shock wasn't entirely convincing. "Where?"

Tansy climbed onto my shoulder. "Don't play games. I know what you've been doing over there."

"You *were* trespassing," said Leona.

"You tried to summon my grandmother's ghost!" I struggled to keep my grip on the fence, but I refused to let her out of my sight. "Was that what you were really doing in the woods near my mum's house? Gathering herbs for a summoning?"

Her face flushed like a neon cocktail from the Fox's Den. "You can't prove anything."

"Question is," I went on, "why exactly were you summoning her?"

"To cover your tracks?" Tansy suggested. "Or to ask *her* if your coven can take ownership of the maze?"

"You can't accuse me of doing anything without proof," she insisted. "I'll tell Tiffany."

"Go right ahead." My aching hands gave way, and I dropped off the fence, landing in the mud.

"Robin?" Ramsey approached me, looking between me and the fence with an expression of confusion on his face. "What are you doing? I heard a crash."

"Someone threw a branch at me." I pointed over my shoulder to the spot where the large oak branch had crushed the hedge bordering the Henbane witches' garden.

"Not Grandma's ghost?" He walked over to the fallen branch and studied it. "A ghost would have to be strong to move that."

"Precisely my thinking." Ignoring Tansy's reprimands from behind me, I tried to lift the branch off the hedge. The solid wood was hard to shift, and an odd smell emanated from it which hadn't been obvious before, like crushed garlic. Our magic didn't smell like garlic. Did the Henbane witches', though?

Ramsey reached for the branch and helped me move it

aside, revealing the squashed hedge and the outline of Leona on the other side of the fence. "Leona, is it? What are you doing over there?"

"Your sister just accused me of attempted murder," Leona said.

"No, *I* accused her of *actual* murder," said Tansy.

"She tried to summon Grandma's ghost," I explained. "I caught her gathering herbs for a summoning spell behind our garden. Then Tansy saw the actual spell through the downstairs window."

"That's right," said Tansy.

Ramsey exhaled. "All right. Leona, I'm going to have to ask you to let me search the property."

"You don't have the authority!" She raised her chin. "Tiffany would never allow it."

"Yes, I do," said Ramsey. "And I have the leader of the Wildwood Coven as my backup."

Relief shot through me. He believed me. Not that Mum would be happy if she found out, but for once, he didn't ask for her permission before leading the way to the building next to ours.

While the Henbane Coven's base was bigger than the average house, it paled in comparison to the Wildwood Coven's headquarters and had only two floors. Since Ramsey didn't tell me not to follow him, I took that as an invitation. Besides, I'd rather one of us went along with him in case the Henbane witches cornered Ramsey when he was alone in their headquarters.

After the incident with the branch, I wouldn't put anything past them.

Leona kept up a steady stream of objections while

Ramsey searched the lower floor. "What room did you see the summoning spell in?"

"I *knew* she was spying on me!" Leona said.

"I wouldn't have needed to if you hadn't interfered with my grandmother's ghost." I led Ramsey to the room whose window overlooked the back garden, but when he entered, no signs of the summoning spell remained. Not so much as a single leaf lay on the table.

The Henbane witches had removed the evidence. "What did you do with the spell?"

"There is no spell," Leona said. To my brother, she added, "I told you she was lying."

"Is there anyone else in here?" Ramsey asked.

"No. They take Fridays off."

"How generous of Tiffany."

"She treats her coven members well, unlike some people." Leona watched Ramsey as he walked out into the corridor, while I hovered awkwardly in the background. From her smug expression, she knew he wouldn't find anything. She'd hidden every trace of the spell.

My brother frowned at me. "I can't arrest anyone based on your word alone, you know. There's no proof."

I know. Even the ghost remained hidden, and I tried not to feel too defeated when I followed my brother out the front door.

When I heard Leona's footsteps behind us, I shot a glare over my shoulder at her. "You *did* hide the evidence. If it turns out you banished my grandmother, then you'll face the wrath of the future Head Witch."

"I'd be careful what you say," she said. "The future Head Witch hasn't been chosen, and your coven might not be on top for much longer."

"What makes you so sure?"

"You don't even notice what happens under your own nose, do you?" she goaded. "Ask your cousin Rowan where she's been spending her time lately."

I halted in mid-step. "Think of a better lie next time."

"It isn't a lie," she said. "She never showed up to the Head Witch ceremony for a reason. She was taking our loyalty test."

"Your *what?*" How could she possibly know what Rowan had been doing while the rest of us had been waiting for the new Head Witch to be chosen?

A defiant expression appeared on her face. "When she applied to join the Henbane witches, she needed to prove she renounced her old coven. We gave her several tests."

"You're seriously pushing your luck here, you know." I looked for Ramsey, only to see he'd already returned to the Wildwood Coven's headquarters. "Rowan wouldn't turn her back on our coven."

"Tiffany told me not to tell you, but I don't care any longer. She's the one who did that interview with the *Blue Moon*'s reporters."

Rowan had spoken to the press? No way. Rowan might not get along with her mother and sister, but she'd never screw over the rest of us.

Would she?

What had she been doing near the maze earlier? Why had she come here if she'd been trying to avoid her family?

And if nobody else in the family had been behind the interview, then Rowan was the sole person I hadn't considered yet.

She's lying. She must be lying.

"Robin?" Tansy said anxiously. "What's wrong?"

"Rowan." I'd lost sight of my youngest cousin after I'd spoken to Leona, so I had assumed she'd gone home to avoid her mother and sister. "Leona said she talked to the press."

I picked up the pace and speed-walked down the road, into the alley between our houses, and scrambled up the drainpipe.

"Robin!" Tansy called to me from the fence. "If it's true, I don't think you should go into her house."

"I have to know." I reached the windowsill and straightened upright, belatedly giving the signal when I saw Rowan was in her room.

She startled when she spotted me. "Robin. Hang on…"

Rowan pushed the window open wider, but I didn't enter, instead holding onto the window frame with one hand and looking at her through the glass. "Did you talk to the press, Rowan?"

"Did I what?" Her face reddened, while Ralph detached himself from his web and landed on her shoulder. "Who said that?"

"Leona told me," I said. "You don't actually want to join the Henbane Coven, do you?"

Her mouth hung open for a second. "She *told* you? I thought—"

"But is it true?"

She lowered her gaze. "I can't stay in this house a moment longer. Joining another coven is my only way out. You can't lie and pretend they'll miss me."

"You mean your mum and sister," I said. "*I'll* miss you. Besides, did they really tell you to badmouth your family to the press in order to be allowed in?"

Her flush deepened. "My mum and sister deserve all the bad press they get."

"The *Blue Moon* printed a story saying that Grandma was murdered and that my *mother* was the main suspect," I pointed out. "And my brother blamed me for it."

"I didn't know you'd be blamed," she protested. "I didn't tell them Grandma was murdered—"

"If you so much as hinted that she was, they could have come up with the rest themselves." Disbelief flooded me. "I thought you knew that."

"I had to." Her hands clenched at her sides. "You don't know what it's been like living in this house. I had to escape."

"You're a legal adult, Rowan. What's stopping you from getting a job outside of the coven?"

"My mum already cut off my allowance as soon as I turned eighteen," she said. "If I didn't work for the coven, I'd have nothing."

"You should have told me." Or rather, I should have guessed from all the times she'd turned down my offers of help finding work outside of Wildwood Heath. "Why does she want you to work for the coven so badly? You're not the eldest."

"No, I'm the spare." Her voice cracked. "She told me straight out that she expects me and Vanessa to balance out *your* side of the family and make sure your mother doesn't have too much influence over the council."

"She's coven leader, Rowan," I said. "Also, Ramsey isn't on the council, and neither am I."

"Exactly." She grimaced. "There's no point in me playing her games any longer, but joining the Henbane witches is my only way out. Don't take that away from me too."

I stared numbly at her, my heart sinking in my chest. I hadn't known things had deteriorated that badly with her family, but I felt like a fool for not considering sooner that she might have gone to desperate measures to escape them.

"Robin!" Ramsey's voice cut through the air, almost causing me to lose my balance. "What *are* you doing up there?"

"Hang on." I climbed down the drainpipe and hopped back into the alley between our houses, while Tansy scurried up onto my shoulder. "Ramsey—she did the interview. Rowan did. She told the press that Grandma was murdered."

Surprise flickered through his features. Then I saw who stood behind him... Mum. Her own expression was inscrutable. If I had to guess, Ramsey had told her about our failed attempt to search the Henbane Coven's base for evidence of a summoning spell. Dread trickled down my spine as Mum beckoned both of us into the house and firmly closed the door behind us.

"Rowan did the interview, did she?" Mum asked. "Who told you that?"

"Leona, but Rowan herself admitted the truth." I walked into the living room, but I remained standing instead of taking a seat. "Turns out she wants to join the Henbane Coven herself to get away from her scheming mother and sister. Tiffany said she needed to prove her loyalty."

"So she spoke to the *Blue Moon*'s reporters," Ramsey concluded. "That explains where it started."

"Aren't you going to go and yell at her like you did me?" An apology would have been nice too. "And Tiffany, who told her to speak to them in the first place?"

Ramsey grimaced. "The press interview was the more important issue before Grandma came back from the dead. Now, finding her ghost is the priority."

"The Henbane witches already have grounds to accuse us of harassing them," Mum said. "You shouldn't have gone to search their headquarters without any proof."

"There *was* proof before they hid it," I pointed out.

"You should have known better than to follow Robin's lead, Ramsey."

Okay, that was unfair. "Tansy and I saw Leona gathering herbs for a ghost summoning behind our garden."

"That's not proof either," Ramsey said. "Sorry, Mum. It won't happen again."

"I notice you haven't apologised to *me* for accusing me of telling tales." I folded my arms across my chest, but not in time to hide the glow of magic at my fingertips. Both Horace and Carmilla woke from their naps and hissed, while Ramsey and Mum exchanged glances. "Would you have any regrets if the branch had actually crushed me to death?"

"What branch?" Mum gave me a sharp look. "What did you do this time?"

"What did *I* do?" I echoed. "I didn't drop a branch on my own head, but someone did. Ramsey, you saw the size of that thing."

"The oak tree," said Ramsey, his face turning an even deeper shade of crimson. "Yes, and I'd like to know why you were climbing on the hedges to begin with. To see into the Henbane Coven's garden?"

Mum's expression turned flinty. "How exactly did you find out they had a spell set up for a summoning? Did you sneak into their garden yourself?"

"Are we forgetting the attempted murder part?" How could Mum sweep my near-death experience aside so casually? Okay, she and Ramsey hadn't witnessed the moment the branch had fallen... but Rowan had been there. She couldn't have been responsible, though... could she? "Look, I didn't think anyone would take Tansy's word for it alone, and besides, I wanted to see if Grandma's ghost was there as well."

"She wasn't," Ramsey said unnecessarily. "If they did try a summoning, it didn't work."

"Something caused her to vanish." I gave Carmilla a beseeching look, but the cat hardly seemed to care that we were talking about the ghost of her witch. "Leona broke the law. Twice over if she was the one who dropped the branch on me."

"Again—no proof." Mum released a breath. "Is there anything else you forgot to mention?"

"I smelled someone's magic on the branch," I recalled. "It was kind of like... garlic cloves."

"Garlic?" she repeated. "I don't know of anyone whose magic smells like that."

"Neither do I," Ramsey said. "It won't hold up as evidence."

"How convenient." My anger was directed at myself as much as Ramsey. I shouldn't have assumed Leona would leave evidence of the summoning lying around, not after she'd realised Tansy and I had been peering through the windows. "Where did Aunt Shannon and Vanessa go?"

"Home, and it's lucky they didn't see you scaling the

wall like that squirrel of yours." Mum tutted. "They spent a fair amount of time trying to convince me to let them take the sceptre home for safekeeping."

My brows shot up. "Like you'd fall for that one."

Aunt Shannon needed to face the consequences of what she'd done. Even if she hadn't been involved in Grandma's death, the way she'd treated Rowan was unfair enough that I understood why she'd snapped. But if *she'd* knocked the branch down… no, it couldn't have been her. Rowan might be unhappy with the coven, but she didn't want *me* dead, right?

Unnerved, I went into the back garden to seek some privacy and talk to my familiar. The garden was as calm as ever despite the slightly wild state of the roses. Piper would have a lot of cleaning up to do when Mum let her come back to work.

Tansy resumed her attack on the bird feeders, but her efforts seemed half-hearted, and she soon returned to my side. "What's wrong? You don't think Rowan was the one who dropped that branch on you, do you?"

"I don't think so, but it wasn't an accident." If not Leona, then who else? "Unless Grandma's poltergeist skills went out of control."

"She might have been aiming for Leona."

"She'd have shown her face." Yet she'd hidden herself away as soon as she'd escaped Mum and me. Now Aunt Shannon was even madder at us, and I'd bet she'd take it out on her daughter. Did I really blame her for being willing to do anything to escape?

The cruel stories the press had printed weren't easy to forget, but it was Tiffany who'd pressured Rowan into talking to the reporters. It was a great way to kill two birds with one stone: disgrace my family in the public eye *and* take one of the Wildwood witches under her wing. And if she could make Rowan betray me in the process, so much the better.

Tansy wrapped her fluffy tail around the back of my neck. "She'll come back."

"That's what concerns me. She didn't even say anything to identify her killer." A sudden suspicion hit me. "Did *she* bring Grandma's ghost back in the first place? Rowan, I mean?"

"Why would Rowan summon her?" asked Tansy.

"I don't know, but—she wasn't at the ceremony." And Leona hadn't specified *what* she'd been doing to prove her loyalty to the Henbane witches. "It makes sense."

"You don't think her ghost came back on her own?" she said. "You know your grandmother's strong enough to have come back from death if she wanted to."

"True, but the timing was suspicious." Not that I had any proof. "Never mind. Mum and Ramsey would never believe me anyway."

"I can sneak around your aunt's house and look for the evidence." Tansy leapt off my shoulder onto the grass.

"Do you want to get her into trouble with Aunt Shannon, though?" My aunt might have been more bark than bite, but she'd driven Rowan into betraying her coven, and I wasn't sure there was a way to reverse the damage she'd done.

Rowan's situation made my own family problems look minor by comparison, and talking to the press didn't mean she was responsible for dropping the branch on my head. Or rather, I didn't *want* her to be the one responsible.

Despite knowing who was responsible for the interview, though, we were further from answers about Grandma's murderer than ever. And with Grandma's ghost nowhere to be seen, that didn't look set to change anytime soon.

13

When Piper messaged me, asking if I wanted to meet up at the Fox's Den, I agreed in an instant. We sat at the same table as the last time, where I proceeded to bring her up to date on recent events. Of course, she'd witnessed Grandma's ghost's appearance like everyone else had, but she'd obeyed Mum's directive not to come near the coven's headquarters until the spirit had been taken care of and had therefore missed everything else.

She believed me without hesitation when I told her about Leona's antics.

"So you think the Henbane Coven might have tried to have you killed?" she asked. "As well as summoning your grandmother's ghost?"

"And recruiting my cousin." I stabbed my straw into my cocktail and gave it a stir. "Ah, it was Rowan who actually summoned her ghost in the first place, I think."

"Poor thing," Piper commented. "I'd be inclined to

place the blame on your Aunt Shannon's head, personally."

"I should have figured out she wasn't above forcing her own children to support her bid for the title of coven leader." I sipped at my drink. "Rowan's in enough trouble as it is, and besides, Mum and I summoned Grandma as well."

"You did?"

"Before she went full poltergeist." Nobody could control Grandma's ghost. Not the Henbane Coven or even my own family. "I think Mum regrets letting me summon her at all."

"Wow, she went ahead with one of your ideas?" Piper ordered another drink. "I guess if she thinks her mother was murdered, then she's willing to do anything to find the culprit."

"I think she suspected all along," I murmured. "Grandma doesn't remember her death, though. She died in her sleep."

"Didn't she live in your mum's house, though?" Piper frowned. "You'd think she'd have searched her rooms."

"I bet that's the first thing she did before dismissing the staff."

Her eyes rounded with understanding. "Oh. *That's* why she got so paranoid and wouldn't let me into the house."

"I doubt she thinks *you* did it," I said hastily. "You didn't have access to her rooms."

"Or a death wish," Piper added. "Have you looked around the scene of her death?"

"No, but I assume Mum took note of any clues if she found them." Not that she'd been willing to share any of her ideas with me. "It took her long enough to admit the

Head Witch's death wasn't accidental. She practically bit my head off the first time I made the suggestion."

Piper pursed her lips. "Does she have any suspects?"

"She and Aunt Shannon have been firing the blame at one another, but I can't tell how much of that was due to their rivalry over the coven leadership."

All the same, I'd dearly have liked to know what she and Grandma had argued about prior to her death… and what evidence she might have found and not shared with me.

"What about the Henbane Coven, then?" she asked. "Have you spoken to Tiffany since Leona revealed she recruited your cousin?"

"No, but she wasn't around," I said. "I didn't see anyone else in their headquarters, so only Leona could have dropped that branch on my head."

Her… or Rowan. My thoughts rebelled against blaming my cousin, but did I really know Rowan? She'd summoned a ghost and trounced my family's reputation in an interview without seeming to care if the entire town realised the Head Witch had been murdered… and that even the rest of her coven had yet to find the person responsible.

I cast a surreptitious look around the pub, wondering how many people in here might be talking about the coven's gossip. I'd hoped to run into Harvey again, too, but he was nowhere to be seen, and he hadn't messaged me since I'd turned him down yesterday. If I had to guess, I'd blown my chance. I did spot Stacy slumped in a chair near the window, looking pretty miserable herself. No surprise given that she was out of a job.

Piper prodded me under the table. "Lighten up. Look,

if you want to get proof of the Henbane Coven's trickery, you can always sneak into their headquarters and look for yourself."

"Do I really need to get into any more trouble?" I shook my head. "Leona put the spell away. Grandma's ghost never showed up."

"Nobody is going to be there at night," she reminded me. "We have *magic,* besides, remember?"

"I think you're a little drunk." Then again, I was halfway there myself, and after several cocktails, going along with Piper's plan felt like an excellent idea.

Not long before the pub closed for the night, we made our way back towards our coven's territory. Piper pulled out her wand and cast unseen spells on both of us which would enable us to walk around without being spotted by anyone who didn't already know we were there. The disadvantage to being both drunk and semi-invisible became apparent when we lost sight of one another before we'd even reached the Henbane Coven's headquarters.

When I reached the right place, however, it was the building next door which drew my attention. A light shone in the window of one of the downstairs classrooms in the Wildwood Coven's headquarters. Mum had warded the doors... so who could be in there?

"Piper, are you there?" I whispered. "See that light?"

Was it Grandma's ghost? I trod closer and tripped over someone on the doorstep—someone invisible. The person yelped, a high-pitched noise which didn't disguise their identity.

"Leona." What was she doing outside the Wildwood

Coven's headquarters? I grabbed her invisible shoulders before she could run off.

"Let me go!" she yelped.

"You're trying to get at the sceptre," Piper slurred from behind me. "Aren't you?"

"Or Grandma's ghost," I added.

"I have no idea what you're talking about!" Leona tried to wriggle out of my grip again, but I'd unintentionally landed on top of her invisible cloak when I'd tripped and planted both feet on the end. "I'm not interested in ghosts."

"Then why were you breaking in?" Piper asked. "Don't deny it. There's no reason for you to be on *our* coven's doorstep."

"Do you want me to hand you over to my brother?"

"No!" She struggled, then the fight went out of her. "I didn't want to fight with you. Tiffany told me to."

"Did she tell you to pressure Rowan into lying to the press about her own family?" I asked. "Or was that Tiffany's doing too?"

"It's all her," she mumbled. "I'm only her apprentice."

Rowan isn't going to have a better time with the Henbane witches than with her own family. I had to tell her, but would she be willing to listen to me? "She's still supposed to respect you. Did she make you summon my grandmother's ghost?"

"No… that was me."

"I knew it," Piper said triumphantly. "What were you doing, trying to banish her to hide the evidence of her murder?"

"No!" Her shrill exclamation was accompanied by another lunge for freedom, but she succeeded only in doing an invisible face-plant on the doorstep. "No, I… I'm a dud. A magical dud."

"You're a what?" That couldn't be right. "Why'd you try to summon Grandma's ghost if you knew it wouldn't work?"

"I was desperate." Her voice cracked. "Tiffany told me… she told me the sceptre might be able to fix me."

"The sceptre's not going to pick someone without magic." I'd never *seen* her use magic, admittedly, but who else had tried to drop that branch on my head? "You summoned Grandma… why?"

"To ask for a trial with the sceptre," she said. "I assumed she didn't want anyone in her family to have it, but she always had a soft spot for witches who struggled with magic. Like that assistant of hers."

"She wouldn't have given it to you," Piper said. "I think you're lying."

"If you can't use magic, how do you explain the branch?" I queried.

"I didn't do that," Leona insisted. "And I don't know who did."

Only one other person had been near the maze. Had my cousin truly tried to have me killed? My head pounded, while Leona flickered into visibility again. Her spell must have worn off.

"Please let me go," she said.

"Not so fast," said Piper. "Who spelled you invisible if you can't use magic?"

"I brewed a potion," she said. "I can do that, but wand-based spells are what give me trouble. It's more common than you'd think."

"Give me one reason not to turn you in." Except for

the fact that Ramsey was off duty tonight, that is, but Leona hadn't actually broken into the coven's headquarters. I doubted she'd have made it past the wards.

A light flashed in the window. My head snapped up, but the light had already winked out by the time I focused on the coven's headquarters. Leona, meanwhile, gave a desperate tug on her robe and pulled herself free.

"Stop!" Piper gave chase down the road, but the teenage witch was surprisingly fast, and two drunken, semi-invisible people were at a distinct disadvantage. Piper barely made it a few metres before stopping to throw up in a bush.

"I think I've lost my wand," she mumbled when she raised her head.

"I'll help you find it." I turned back to the coven's headquarters, but the light in the window had gone out. I crept over to the door and checked that the ward remained intact, which it did. Had Mum been responsible for turning on the light? Or the ghost? Nobody else could bypass the wards, or so I thought. Including Leona.

Regardless, I made a mental note to send Ramsey after her as soon as I'd got Piper home.

————

The following morning brought another hangover from hell and no potion this time. I'd have to brew my own but no potion would get rid of my lingering sense of guilt.

I probed my memories to figure out why. I'd caught the person who'd summoned Grandma's ghost and badmouthed the family to the press, but in Rowan's position, I might have done the same. For all our mutual commiserating over our terrible family luck, I'd never asked her how it felt being stuck in that house with no way out.

As for Leona, Piper and I never had managed to find her after she'd taken off yesterday. When I went downstairs and found Ramsey in the kitchen, I was deeply confused for a second before I remembered he wasn't at work today because it was the weekend.

I had less than two days before I was supposed to return to my regular life, but Grandma's killer had yet to be found, and the idea of leaving my family in such a mess felt like turning my back on a burning house.

"I've arrested her," Ramsey said to me by way of a "good morning."

"What?" I rubbed my sore head. "Who?"

"Rowan," said Prickles, who sat on the table beside his owner.

"What do you mean, you've arrested her?" I hadn't sent him after her last night, had I? I didn't recall seeing him in the house after my return from helping Piper get home, but I assumed that if he'd gone after anyone, it'd be Leona.

"She confessed to summoning the ghost of our grandmother," Ramsey said. "As a result, she's the main suspect for Grandma's murder."

My heart sank, and a wave of nausea crashed over me. "She confessed? Why?"

"What you said yesterday reminded me that she hadn't been questioned yet," he explained. "And that she wasn't present at the ceremony when Grandma's ghost first showed up."

My mouth went dry. "I thought you needed evidence."

"And we found it," he said. "That is, I sent my team to

search her room, and they found the remnants of the summoning spell in her room."

Tansy. I'd sent her to spy on my cousin. Had she unearthed the evidence in the process? My familiar was less inclined to feel sorry for Rowan than I was, though I had to admit that turning herself in might have been an act of self-preservation before Aunt Shannon had inevitably found out.

I slumped into a seat. "She was trapped in that house. I bet she'd rather be in jail."

"I did get that impression." He gave me a sideways look. "I thought you didn't agree with what she did, though."

"Just because I don't agree with what she did doesn't mean I don't understand why she did it." I rested my head in my hands. "Leona too. She told me when I ran into her last night that Tiffany was pulling her strings."

"Last night?" He climbed to his feet. "You never mentioned seeing her last night."

"I thought I might have told you when I got in."

Prickles cleared his throat. "When you got in, you fell asleep in the hall. Ramsey had to carry you up to bed."

Oops. "Piper and I tripped over Leona outside the coven's headquarters. She'd used an invisibility potion and was trying to get through the wards. Unsuccessfully."

His brow furrowed. "Is this the same as your claim yesterday that she had a summoning spell inside the Henbane Coven's base? Because I can't storm into her property again."

"It was *our* coven's property she was trying to break into," I said. "Besides, she admitted that she's a magical dud and was trying to steal the sceptre in the hopes that it'd help her."

"How drunk were you, exactly?"

"I'm telling the truth." He didn't believe me? Seriously? "Oh—I also saw a light in one of the downstairs windows of the coven's headquarters."

"Robin, when I found you sleeping in the hall last night, you called me Carmilla and tried to climb the stairs backwards."

I groaned into my hands. "Ramsey, I swear I'm telling the truth. If Leona's a dud, it explains why the Henbane witches were trying to recruit people from *our* coven, right?"

"I'm not getting involved this time," he said over his shoulder as he left the kitchen.

I lifted my head, and Prickles hopped off the table to join his owner. *Great.*

My phone buzzed in my pocket. My heart swooped when I saw Harvey had messaged me. I hadn't drunkenly texted him yesterday, had I? I hoped not, but I'd been disappointed not to see him at the Fox's Den. I opened the message, relief washing over me when I found that I hadn't messaged him since my reply to his invitation to join him at the pub two days ago.

Are you free today? his message asked.

Maybe I should have asked him to meet me last night, but it was probably for the best that he hadn't witnessed any of my misadventures with Piper. Given the rate at which I was screwing up lately, he'd be better off staying away, but it'd be unfair of me to take off without a goodbye.

I replied. *I'm free right now, but if you want to go and get coffee from Were's My Coffee?, I'll have to use an invisibility potion if I want to avoid the press.*

No need, came his response. *Meet you at the end of your road in 20 mins?*

Sure. I figured I had nothing to lose at this point, so I passed the time by watching Tansy's ongoing battle over the bird feeders in the garden. Secure in the knowledge that she could keep herself entertained, I went to meet Harvey at the end of the road. He was early, smiling at me with a latte in each hand.

"You're a lifesaver." I reached to take one of the paper cups. "I'd rather not face the press with a hangover."

"You should have mentioned. I'd have got more of that potion."

"That was you?" I definitely should have invited him to join Piper and me last night. If I had to admit it, I'd been ashamed to think that he might see me at my worst or that he might be dragged into my family's problems simply by being around me. Speaking of which, we should probably get out of the open before one of them spotted me. "Want to go for a walk in the woods?"

"Sure." He walked alongside me, and we sipped at our lattes in silence until we reached the forest path which ran behind the row of houses, which pretty much all belonged to prominent members of my coven. "Did you go to the Fox's Den?"

"Yeah." I glanced sideways at him. "I don't normally go out drinking twice in a week, but it's been..."

"Stressful?" he suggested. "A nightmare?"

"Worse." I took another sip of my latte, quickening my pace when we came within sight of the back of Mum's garden. "Oh, yeah... I saw you flying yesterday."

"You saw us practising?" he asked. "I didn't know you were watching or else I'd have waved at you."

"And fallen off your broom?"

"Nah, I haven't done that in a long while," he said. "Do you fly?"

"Not often," I said. "I never tried out for the sports teams, anyway. I wasn't good enough to compete with the best."

"You don't have to play competitively to have fun with something," he said. "Besides, nobody is perfect at everything out of the gate. I fell in a lake during my first flight. Broke both wrists."

"Ouch," I said. "Some people *are* perfect at everything. Like my mother. My brother too."

"Who, the chief of police?"

"That's him." The reviving effect of the latte was fading already. "He might not hold his perfect status for much longer if my aunt hexes him for arresting her daughter."

"If your aunt *what?*" He came to a halt. "Your brother arrested your cousin? Which one?"

"Rowan." I knew Ramsey would be furious at me for telling Harvey, but I needed to vent, and Piper was sleeping off her hangover from the night before. Before I could question my decision, it all came spilling out. "My aunt won't hex him, though. She thinks Rowan's the *spare* and isn't worth the effort."

"Hold on a second," Harvey said. "The last thing I heard was that your grandmother's ghost came back and interrupted the coven leadership ceremony..."

"Yeah, and then she disappeared," I said. "I talked my mother into summoning her again so we could figure out how to get rid of her, but it didn't work. Then I found out the Henbane Coven tried to summon her as well, so Ramsey and I went to confront them only to find they'd hidden the evidence."

His forehead wrinkled in confusion. "So how did your cousin end up getting arrested?"

"Turns out she was the one who told tales on us to the press which led to them writing that article the other day," I said. "She also summoned Grandma's ghost in the first place."

"Neither of those things is a crime… is it?" he asked. "Granted, I'm not entirely certain on the nuances of coven laws. They make Sky Hopper's rules look simple."

"You aren't wrong." Of course, he didn't know Grandma's death hadn't been an accident, and I hadn't even mentioned the falling tree branch yet. Or that Rowan might have been responsible for both. "My brother doesn't handle humiliation well, and he's been furious that someone blabbed our secrets to the press. He accused *me* of doing it at first."

"He did what?" The indignation in his tone was gratifying, I wouldn't lie.

"He blamed me, but in his defence, I did do an interview with the press when I was a teenager and I didn't know any better," I said. "I hoped we'd reached a truce, but then I asked him to come and find evidence of the Henbane Coven's involvement in summoning Grandma's ghost. After that dead end, he said he's not going to bother listening to me again."

"That's hardly fair," he said. "You couldn't have known the coven would hide the evidence of their summoning spell, could you?"

"I should have guessed they would." I rubbed my forehead with my free hand. "See, this is a prime example of why I don't get involved in the coven's business. It only ends in disaster."

"Robin," he said, "I can't pretend I know what's going on with your family, but it's not up to you to fix their problems. Not when they don't seem to appreciate you in the slightest."

I blinked. "You think I should leave?"

"I think you should make the decision for yourself, not for them."

Easier said than done. The coven's hold over my life went beyond my family's obligations. Like my connection to the Wildwood, the magic flowing under the surface which linked me to the source of my power. Cutting myself off from my home entirely didn't appeal, but I had to convince my family to meet me halfway if I wanted us to get anywhere.

"Also," he added, "if you want an escape route after this is over, I have a broomstick you can borrow."

I laughed. "I'm good, really. But thanks."

14

Meeting with Harvey had improved my mood, but my worries began to seep back in when I returned to the house to find Mum and Dad having a raging argument on the doorstep.

"What do you mean, she's gone?" Dad said. "You let her go wandering off alone when there's a murderer on the loose?"

I cleared my throat. "If you mean me, I'm right here."

"There you are, Robin." He swept me into a hug. "Your mother decided to finally tell me someone tried to have you killed yesterday. Why are you still wandering around on your own?"

"I wasn't alone. I met someone in the woods," I said to both of them, feeling a mixture of guilt and defiance. "Besides, I can take care of myself."

Dad's expression crumpled. "I know you can, but your mother said you were out until the early hours of the morning."

"I was with a friend," I said. "You know, Piper, the

coven's gardener. I was doing fine until I woke up and found out Ramsey arrested Rowan, of all people, for Grandma's murder."

"Robin," Mum said. "That's not why she was arrested."

"Summoning a ghost isn't a crime." I glanced up at Aunt Shannon's house, but the curtains were pulled closed. "He wouldn't listen to me when I told him that Piper and I ran into Leona last night by the coven's headquarters—"

"Are you going to explain why you and Piper were drunkenly wandering the street, then?" asked Mum.

"Wait, was it *you* I saw in there?" I asked. "The light in the window?"

"No," she said. "What did you say about Leona?"

"She was trying to break through the wards to our coven's headquarters," I said. "Turns out she's a dud, without any magic talent, and she wanted to steal the sceptre."

"That," Mum said, "is ridiculous."

"Ramsey didn't believe me, but Leona herself can back me up," I said. "Tiffany is as bad as Aunt Shannon for bullying her apprentices. It was her who pressured Rowan into doing that interview."

"That is no excuse." Mum's voice tightened with anger. "If you're telling the truth—"

"Of course she is," Dad said. "Robin wouldn't lie about something so important. Her own safety is at stake."

"Not just mine," I put in. "I know Ramsey is under pressure, but Rowan isn't the killer."

"She summoned my mother's ghost," Mum said. "And disrupted the ceremony."

"Tiffany must have told her to." Why, though? To mess

with our coven and cast doubt on Mum's fitness for the position of Head Witch? She'd succeeded on both counts, but something still wasn't quite right about the timing of Grandma's ghost's appearance. "Not sure why…?"

Mum's steely expression betrayed nothing. "To undermine our family, of course."

But who? Rowan would never have wanted her mother to gain the position of Head Witch, but stopping Mum from claiming the title had done nothing but stir up discord. My memory drifted back to the light I'd seen in the window last night. If it hadn't been Mum or Ramsey, that left Vanessa or Aunt Shannon as the most likely culprits.

Why would they have been sneaking around there at night? Had they been after the sceptre or searching for Grandma's ghost?

"I should go," Dad said as if picking up on the fury lurking behind Mum's calm eyes. "Stay safe, okay?"

"Of course." I hugged him goodbye, and when I next looked for Mum, I spotted her approaching the coven's headquarters. I caught her up partway down the road. "What are you doing?"

"I'm going to speak to Tiffany," she said. "I wonder if she'll be in at the weekend."

"What are you going to say?" I wanted to know what excuse she might make for her apprentice, but while Leona had confessed her plan, I hadn't actually got hold of any physical evidence to speak of. With only Piper—who'd been drunk at the time—to back up my word, the evidence looked pretty flimsy in daylight. "Leona and Tiffany have probably concocted a cover story after she got caught. Besides, Ramsey isn't around."

He didn't believe me—but either Mum did or she had her own grievances to air, because she didn't respond to my question. Instead, she made straight for the Henbane Coven's headquarters and knocked on the door twice.

Tiffany answered, wearing her usual bright robes and none of the falsely friendly manner she'd had at the funeral. "I do hope you've come to apologise for yesterday's baseless accusation."

"It wasn't baseless," I said. "Leona was trying to do a summoning spell even if she wasn't successful. I *saw* her."

"You're willing to confess to trespassing, then, are you?"

"Only if you admit that one of your people tried to drop a branch on my head."

"None of my coven's members did anything of the sort."

"Someone did." I pointed at the oak tree. "That giant branch came crashing down straight after I went to look for the summoning spell. Leona is a magical dud, she told me, so who was hiding in the garden? I'm guessing they helped themselves to the same invisibility potion Leona used."

Tiffany's eyes narrowed. "Don't you dare say that about my apprentice again."

"About being a dud?" I asked. "She told me herself when I caught her trying to break into *our* property to steal the sceptre. Or are you denying she has no magical skill?"

"It's easy enough to check," said Mum. "I assume it's on her academy record."

Tiffany's face flushed. "It's none of your business what skill my apprentice has. I happen to think my coven members have value beyond their magical prowess, unlike you, which is how we managed to gain the trust of your niece."

Rowan. She wasn't part of the Henbane Coven yet, but she'd been visiting them. Had she been using the potion too? Had it been her I'd seen inside the coven's headquarters last night?

Did she drop that branch on me?

No. She might have been desperate, but she wouldn't do that. Right?

"That is not what I think at all," said Mum. "My sister and I diverge on some key points, and we certainly don't encourage theft. You do realise that stealing the sceptre is worth a life sentence, don't you?"

"You have no proof." The merest tremor entered her voice. "This won't stand."

"Did you think I wouldn't take my daughter's word for it?" Mum said. "You're mistaken."

I stared at her in disbelief. Mum knew I'd been drunk last night, and in only Piper's company, but she believed me where even Ramsey hadn't. "Does anyone in your coven use magic which smells of garlic?"

"Garlic?" echoed Tiffany. "No, they don't. If this is a new accusation, then I don't appreciate it."

"Just checking." I took a step backwards as she closed the door with a snap. "I'm guessing she's off to hide any incriminating evidence in case you send Ramsey to search the place again."

"She can't hide Leona's record," said Mum. "She's a minor, so she wouldn't face the full force of the magical law for attempting to steal the sceptre, but it's not something she wants on her record."

"No." I looked away. "Don't you want to ask Piper to back up my story?"

"Robin, you might have made mistakes on occasion, but you've never lied to me about anything important."

It took everything I had not to ask if she was pulling my leg. "I didn't exactly help with the ghost situation. Or finding the Henbane witches guilty."

"I think Tiffany will reflect on her mistakes." She turned her back and swept towards home, while I frowned after her for a moment. She hadn't indicated that she believed Rowan to be guilty either way, but if she'd thought Tiffany was responsible for her mother's death, she would have come right out and accused her, surely.

Despite the recent ways in which Mum had unexpectedly taken my side, I couldn't forget that she had yet to tell me everything that had transpired since Grandma's death, nor the events leading up to her passing. And with my quest for answers sent spiralling back to the start, my last option was to question my immediate family.

Mum walked in silence, while my heart began to beat faster when we neared the house. I had to find out what she knew, however little I might want to hear it.

As we entered the house, I tailed her into the living room. "Whose magic *does* smell of garlic?"

Mum frowned. "Garlic?"

"The smell was all over that branch that fell on me," I explained. "If Tiffany was telling the truth, then who knocked it down? Was it the same as the person who killed Grandma?"

A heartbeat passed. "No. They couldn't have got into the house."

"If she was murdered, then I have as much right to

investigate as the rest of us do," I said quietly. "I want to find her killer, but we aren't going to get anywhere if we aren't straight with one another. I've told you everything I know, but you were the last person to see her before she died. Weren't you?"

Instead of answering, she went into the kitchen. "I'll make tea. Then I'll tell you."

Mum never made tea, and for good reason. When she handed me my cup and sat in an armchair in the living room, I managed half a sip of lukewarm dusty water, which I spat out before putting down the cup and sitting in another armchair.

"My mother and I argued the night before her death because I was concerned that she was overworking herself," she said. "She was far too old to be constantly travelling around to regional coven meetings as well as running the Wildwood Coven, but she insisted that she'd be chosen as Head Witch again when the time came and that nothing would stop her from keeping the title."

"On Samhain." The Head Witch's title traditionally renewed annually, which meant Grandma's position would have been up for grabs on that day, but it wasn't for several months yet.

Mum yawned as she drank her tea, the cup rattling when she put it down. "I confronted her, but she refused to listen."

"And then?"

"And then she never woke up the next day," she said. "It was a minor disagreement, and your aunt and cousin know it was. They just want an excuse to discredit me."

"But what actually killed her?" I asked. "Do you know?"

"Poison," she said. "A lethal dose. I know the signs, but I found no physical traces in her room. I assume the person responsible gave her the poison before she came home for the night, but it must have been slow-acting enough that it didn't take effect until after she went to bed."

"Poison," I repeated. "You're sure they didn't get into the house?"

"They couldn't have done so without being detected by one of us, but I had to be certain, so I dismissed the household staff until I could be."

"The household staff would have had access to her quarters," I acknowledged. "But you definitely didn't find anything in her rooms?"

"Nor in her office at headquarters," she said. "The killer was careful to cover their tracks."

"Hmm." I raised a brow as she gave another yawn, her eyes drooping. "Are you okay? You haven't slept all week, have you?"

"I'm the new coven leader," Mum said. "I don't have time to rest as long as my predecessor's death remains unsolved."

"You don't have to do it alone," I told her. "Being Head Witch or coven leader doesn't mean you can't ask other people for help. Even Grandma had an assistant."

Her eyes widened a little. Then they slid closed, and abruptly, she fell into a dead sleep, her arm drooping over the side of the chair.

"Mum?" While she *was* obviously sleep deprived, she wasn't the type to randomly doze off. Her teacup hung over the edge of the table, so I rescued it, grimacing as an odd herbal scent hit my nose.

My heart gave a lurch. *Did she accidentally put a potion in her drink?* I ran into the kitchen and checked in the cupboards she'd left open. The teabags looked normal, but when I checked on the milk she'd left out on the side, the strong smell of herbs emanated from the bottle. A sleeping draught… and a strong one too.

"Whose is this?" I asked of nobody in particular.

A yowl sounded. Carmilla sat in the doorway between the kitchen and the hall, what was left of her tufty fur standing on end.

"Carmilla." I put down the bottle. "Can you talk now?"

She opened her mouth and yawned in answer. When the front door opened with a loud click, I damn near jumped out of my skin.

"Robin, is that you?" Ramsey called out.

"Yes, it is." My heart raced erratically, and I turned away from the cat. "We have a situation here."

"What did you do to Mum?" He entered the living room and stared at her sleeping form on the sofa.

"That's what I meant by 'situation.'" I held up the bottle so he could see it. "Someone switched out the milk with a sleeping potion."

"Oh, that's Grandma's," he said. "She must have left it in the fridge. Why did Mum make tea? She never does that."

"What?" I stared at him. "Grandma was using a sleeping potion?"

"Yes, for a while," he said. "Why *did* Mum make tea?"

"Because nobody else is around to make it for her," I said. "You know she's terrible at anything in the kitchen, same as me. I didn't drink any of it, but she did."

He picked up her abandoned teacup and sniffed it.

"That's definitely some kind of sleeping draught. Did she not check?"

"She wasn't paying attention at the time." I studied the bottle, but it had no label, of course. "Who even brewed this? It's strong stuff."

"I thought Grandma had it custom made," he said. "I don't know whose idea it was to put it in a milk bottle."

"Mum said Grandma was under a lot of pressure, but she didn't mention she was regularly taking sleeping draughts." My gaze drifted over to Mum, a sudden suspicion rising in the back of my mind.

"You must have rattled her pretty thoroughly if she wanted to make tea," Ramsey commented. "Though she needs the rest if you ask me. What were you talking about?"

"Grandma." Where was that cat? I looked into the kitchen, but Carmilla had slunk away somewhere when Ramsey had come in. "She just got back from confronting Tiffany, so I'd say she's more to blame for rattling her."

"Tiffany?" His footsteps retreated as he moved around the kitchen, cleaning up the mess Mum's tea-making attempt had left. I, meanwhile, spotted Carmilla sitting on the lowest stair. "Why?"

"Because of what I told you earlier." I approached Carmilla, but she retreated up the stairs, out of my reach. "She recruited Rowan and pressured her into turning against her family, and her apprentice tried to steal the sceptre. But she didn't kill Grandma."

"Who, Rowan? I know she didn't." He exhaled in a sigh. "I know I overreacted when I arrested her, Robin."

Wow. He was actually admitting to making a mistake?

"I don't think Rowan was the killer, but it was someone close to Grandma who poisoned her."

I might not have been top of my class in potion making, but I *did* know that sleeping potions could be lethal if one took too heavy a dose. Slow acting too. With Mum unconscious, it was on me to find the culprit.

15

To start off with, I went in search of Tansy. My familiar came scampering over as soon as I opened the back door. "What's new?"

"A lot," I replied. "I'm going to search Grandma's rooms. Want to come?"

I gave my familiar a brief rundown of that morning's events as we headed upstairs. Carmilla tried to trip me up at the top of the stairs, but she didn't stop me from approaching Grandma's private suite.

Mum must have searched the place, even if she hadn't shared the results with anyone else, but I'd keep an eye out for anything she might have overlooked. All the same, I felt like I was trespassing when I pushed open the door, though Grandma's ghost wasn't anywhere to be seen. Only Carmilla accompanied Tansy and me into the room, meowing plaintively from a corner while we scanned the large bedroom and its adjoining en-suite bathroom. Judging from the layer of dust that covered the polished wooden furniture, nobody had come in here to clean since her death. Mum had acted quickly in dismissing the staff.

But not fast enough to prevent a second murder.

Tessa must have died because she'd figured out who the killer was. There was no other possible reason. Given Grandma's own words about Tessa always getting under her feet, it made sense that she might have stumbled upon the killer. The question was, how had she known the truth when nobody in our family had figured it out?

"Hasn't your mum already searched everywhere?" Tansy asked.

"Yes, but she's out cold, and I didn't get the chance to ask if she actually found any clues." Admittedly, it was a little hard to tell what might count as "suspicious" in the room of a former Head Witch, whose shelves contained all manner of magical trinkets. I examined a watch which showed the moon phases; a lifelike ornament of a miniature unicorn; and a sealed box which didn't seem to have any keyhole. Tomes which sang when I opened them lay on the shelves, colour-changing robes lined her wardrobe, and no traces remained of any sleeping potion, lethal or otherwise.

Tansy jumped off the bedside table, stirring up a cloud of dust in her wake. "I can't smell anything weird."

"Including the sleeping potion?" I asked. "If she took a dose of it the night of her death, Mum must have removed it from the room."

Carmilla meowed and left the room, while I let Tansy run ahead of me before firmly closing the door. From there, I went back downstairs to find Ramsey sitting beside a still-unconscious Mum. "Are you going to tell me what you were doing up there?"

"Looking for clues," I said. "Mum's certain that it was some kind of poison that killed Grandma. An overdose of sleeping potion might have the same effect, but there's no evidence left upstairs, and if there was, Mum never figured out who the killer was."

Which meant the only other place to look for evidence was Grandma's office. With Mum out of commission for the next few hours, someone had to step in.

"Robin," Ramsey said as I made for the door. "What are you doing?"

"I'm going to the coven's headquarters," I said over my shoulder. "Keep an eye on Mum, won't you?"

"Wait." He staggered, tripping over Carmilla when she crossed the room like a fluffy tornado and crashed into my ankles.

"Ow." I caught my balance on the door frame. "What is it? You want to come with me?"

"Meow," said Carmilla.

"Okay, then." I turned to my brother. "You can revive Mum with a potion or a spell, can't you? You're better at that kind of thing than I am."

That was putting it mildly, but a sense of urgency propelled me forwards, and the way Carmilla had snapped into action was just fuel on the fire. Why did she want to come with me? Did she understand I was hunting her witch's killer?

Tansy ran alongside me as I left the house. "What are you thinking this time?"

"I'm thinking we haven't searched Grandma's office yet," I said. "And if our would-be thief decides to come back, then we need to be ready."

Tansy kept pace with me, while Carmilla padded in front of us until we reached the coven's headquarters. The shimmering light on the surface of the door told me Mum had yet to remove the warding spell, but Carmilla simply tapped the surface with her paw, and the door sprang open. Of course the former Head Witch's familiar would be able to get around the wards her master had originally created.

Tansy and I entered the lobby, where silence filled the background as the clues danced around in my mind. Someone close to Grandma had poisoned her. If they'd done so using a high dose of the sleeping potion, then they would have been someone in her inner circle, the handful of people she trusted. The list shrank further when I considered who'd been into her actual office recently… and who might have run into Tessa.

I crossed the lobby to her office and pushed on the door handle, which remained sealed. Carmilla, however, wasn't fazed. She padded past me to the door and gave it a whack with her claw. As with the front doors, it moved inward, revealing an office which had barely changed since Grandma had last used it. Cabinets and shelves stood in rows behind a wooden desk on which several books were piled. A large glass case at the side contained the sceptre, which gleamed even in the darkness. Untouched… and unclaimed.

A crash sounded from the back of the room, and Tansy leapt across the desk and flicked open the cabinet door. Stacy jumped violently, dropping a bag of powdered herbs. "Robin?"

"That's me." I watched Tansy, who stood stiff-backed with her tail in the air. "What're you doing in here?"

"Ah… tidying a few things," she said. "The Head Witch told me to."

"Did she now?" I didn't move from the doorway. While Stacy had always struck me as harmless, I couldn't forget that she'd been in Grandma's inner circle. Over the years, maybe she'd even gained enough trust to brew potions for her. "Her ghost talked to you and not to us?"

"Not you?" she asked. "I thought—you summoned her yesterday."

"You weren't here." I studied her. "She escaped and turned poltergeist. If you're still taking orders from her, then you're wasting your time."

When I took a step towards her, she flinched. "She's Head Witch."

"She's a ghost." *Had* she spoken to Grandma? "What does it matter? Mum would do a perfectly good job as Head Witch. She might even have hired you as her assistant like Grandma did."

She gave a half-shrug, not meeting my eyes, and shuffled away from the cabinet. A clinking sound came from her pocket, and I glimpsed a glass vial peeking out before she one-handedly shoved it out of sight.

"What's that?" asked Tansy. "More poison?"

She gave another flinch. "What do you mean?"

"Was it an accident or not?" I was done hedging around the subject. "I know Grandma was taking sleeping potions which someone brewed for her. Someone like her assistant."

She squeezed her eyes shut. "I didn't mean to. The sleeping potion—I overdid it and didn't realise my mistake until later."

So it's true, then. "Did you mean to kill Tessa too?"

Silence filled the room, while Tansy's tail began to wag. When Stacy didn't answer me, I said, "I bet she figured out what you did and confronted you after the funeral."

She looked down, fiddling with her sleeve. "I couldn't let anyone find out. Imagine what the other covens would think if they found out the Head Witch died in an accident. She wouldn't listen to me."

"So you pushed her into the fountain," I said. "And then when you realised I was on your tail, you tried to drop a branch on my head."

She must have been hiding in the maze, concealed by either a spell or a potion. Given her area of expertise, the latter was more likely. Had she been in here last night too? I guessed so, but what was she trying to achieve by delaying a new Head Witch taking power? She couldn't bring back the dead. And if Grandma hadn't already guessed who her killer was, she would soon.

Stacy drew in a steadying breath then lifted her head to meet my eyes. "The Head Witch would want me to stop you from revealing the truth."

As she raised her wand, Tansy leapt up and crashed into her arm. The smell of garlic filled the room as her spell flew over my shoulder and hit the door, causing it to swing open.

"I can see why you rely on potions instead." I coughed on the pungent smell, hearing Carmilla yowling nearby. "Was it you who made Carmilla unable to talk?"

"She saw me cleaning up after myself." She tried to grab Tansy's tail, but my familiar moved far too quickly for her to reach. "If she gave the game away, it'd have all been for nothing."

"You killed Tessa but not Grandma's familiar?" Her loyalty to the Head Witch prevailed, but I doubted Grandma would appreciate it in the slightest. "I bet you didn't count on her coming back."

"Is that what this is?" Tansy plucked a bottle from her pocket. "Smells like a ghost banishment concoction to me."

Stacy let out a strangled cry and made a wild leap over the desk, dislodging Tansy in the process. As my familiar landed on her feet, Stacy grabbed the handle of the sceptre's glass case. "None of you deserves to wield this except for the Head Witch."

Carmilla yowled loudly, while Stacy let go of the case with a sharp cry when it sprang open of its own accord, the sceptre soaring into the air and towards Grandma's desk. Her ghost appeared, reaching out her hand for the sceptre. "This nonsense has gone on for long enough, Stacy."

Her former apprentice swayed as if she might faint, but the sceptre remained hovering near Grandma's ghostly hand, its usual light dimming. Despite her Head Witch status, her ghost couldn't wield it.

"Grandma," I said. "Did you hear Stacy confess to killing you—and Tessa too?"

Stacy broke into a frantic sprint, but Carmilla and Tansy both tackled her at once. Then the door slammed in its frame when Aunt Shannon entered the room.

"You thief!" She pointed directly at me, eyeing the sceptre floating in the air. "How dare you try to claim the sceptre?"

"I wasn't trying to claim it." I pointed at Stacy, who wriggled out from underneath Tansy and made a break for it through the door Aunt Shannon had left open.

Grandma had other ideas. She gestured with a hand, and a gust of wind swept through the office. Cabinets rattled, and the desk shot forward, straight at the doorway. The desk slammed into my knees, sending me flying head over heels, before knocking Aunt Shannon and Stacy over like skittles.

I groaned. "What the hell, Grandma?"

She hadn't had to knock me over along with the others, but I wasn't entirely certain she was in control of her new poltergeist abilities. Several cabinets spilled their contents on the floor, the sceptre's case fell over, and books thudded off shelves with enough noise to wake the dead.

If, that is, the dead hadn't already been well and truly awake.

"Stop!" I yelled. "Grandma, stop it!"

She didn't seem to hear me. Her ghostly form floated above the centre of the room, while the desk had wedged itself in the doorway with Stacy and Aunt Shannon on the other side. She'd effectively trapped me in the office with a ghost—and the sceptre, which floated near Grandma's transparent hands.

Aunt Shannon climbed onto the desk in an attempt to enter the office again, while Stacy bolted.

"Get back here!" I ran for the door, but Tansy was way ahead of me. A thud sounded when she collided with Stacy from behind, but a single squirrel would have a hard time keeping her restrained even with Carmilla's help. I had to help her.

I called on my magic, reached towards every living creature within range, and shouted, "Stop them!"

Magic exploded from my hands with the force of a

bomb. The windows flew open, and a veritable torrent of birds soared into the office, while small creatures crawled out of the floorboards and converged on both Aunt Shannon and Stacy. Grandma began to laugh, which sounded doubly creepy coming from a ghost.

"Grandma." I staggered towards the desk, my knees throbbing. "That's enough. The police can take over from here."

Ramsey must be able to hear the ruckus. Mum, too, if she'd woken up. I didn't want to mimic Stacy and use a spell to get rid of Grandma. She deserved to choose when she wanted to leave… but the sceptre remained hovering in the air.

Then Aunt Shannon leapt out from beneath a cloud of birds, her face twisted in concentration, and screamed a command. Myrtle the magpie flew through the window and grabbed the sceptre, propelling it towards her hands.

"Wait!" I didn't stop to think. I leapt into the sceptre's path, and my fingers instinctively closed around the end.

At once, its light ignited, a piercing purple colour which spread from my fingertips to my arm.

Aunt Shannon shrieked in fury. "You *cheat!*"

The light continued to glow, while the sceptre vibrated in my hands as waves of shock washed over me. *No. I didn't want this.*

When Aunt Shannon shoved her way into the room, however, my hands moved without my conscious thought. A bolt of purple light shot from the end of the sceptre, sending her crumpling into a heap. Carmilla trod on her face as she padded towards me and sat expectantly at my feet.

Once again, the sceptre lit up, its light washing over

the cat's face. Carmilla opened her mouth and coughed loudly. "Finally. I've been trying to get you to listen to me all week."

"You could understand me." My voice sounded like it belonged to someone else, and the purple glow refused to fade. "Why did you let me stumble around in the dark if you knew who killed your witch?"

"Your mother kept me confined to the house." She padded over to Grandma's ghost. "Besides, I *am* very old."

Grandma studied me. "You? Really?"

"No," I said. "No, it can't be me."

Grandma laughed again, but while I cringed and waited for her retaliation, none came. Even the ghost of the former Head Witch couldn't argue with the sceptre. When she'd finished cackling, she indicated Aunt Shannon's unconscious body on the floor. "Rather you than her."

"No." I shook my head firmly. "I didn't mean to claim the sceptre. I was trying to keep it away from her. Mum's —she drank your sleeping potion by accident."

She gave another laugh. "No accident. We don't need another coven leader working herself to death."

"You know Stacy used the same potion to kill you?" I asked. "By accident?"

"Accident." She tutted. "I suppose it's better than being poisoned by my enemies."

"Grandma, I'm nowhere near qualified to be Head Witch."

"There's no choice," said Grandma. "The sceptre is yours now."

Her words rang in my ears as she vanished into thin

air. A moment later, footsteps sounded, and Ramsey ran into view with Prickles in tow.

Grandma's disembodied laugh echoed in the air, but she didn't reappear. Ramsey's gaze went from Aunt Shannon, who lay sprawled on the floor, to Stacy, pinned beneath an abundance of woodland animals with Tansy sitting triumphantly on her head. I took in a breath and indicated Carmilla. "Want to explain?"

"Meow," said Carmilla.

"She's faking," I told him. "She can talk."

His eyes bulged. "You have the sceptre."

"I didn't steal it."

This would take some explaining.

16

Frankly, I half expected to be poisoned in my sleep by my own mother that night, since she'd remained unconscious for the rest of the day and hadn't responded to Ramsey's attempts at a revival spell. That left it up to the rest of us to deal with cleaning up the aftermath—and since Ramsey's main job was to transport Stacy to jail, that meant I had to do most of it myself. Carmilla, traitor that she was, had found her voice as soon as Ramsey had disappeared and had taken to giving me orders like a pro.

After I collapsed into an exhausted sleep, I woke the following morning when Tansy's tail flicked me on the nose. For a brief moment, I hoped yesterday had been a nightmare. Then my mother walked into the room, holding the sceptre in her hand.

I scrambled upright in bed. "Guess you heard."

"I did." Her expression betrayed nothing as she laid the sceptre down at the end of my bed. "You caught the former Head Witch's killer, and it seems that when you did that, the sceptre found you worthy of being its next wielder."

My chest tightened. "It shouldn't have been me. If you hadn't been knocked out cold, you would have…"

"I didn't even think of Stacy potentially being the killer," she said. "A major oversight on my part. She was such a sweet girl."

"Grandma's death was an accident… but Tessa's wasn't." My hands clenched. "Ramsey arrested her. She's in jail, right?"

"Yes, she is," Mum said. "Accidental or not, the price for killing the Head Witch is steep."

I gave Tansy a stroke when she scampered into my lap. "She didn't want it to go public. Stacy, I mean. She thought the Head Witch being poisoned by accident would damage the coven's reputation."

"So that's why she was willing to commit murder to cover her tracks," she said. "Tragic, really, that she held the coven's reputation foremost in her mind."

"I would find it more tragic if she hadn't tried to kill *me.*" I swung my legs over the edge of the bed, while Tansy scampered onto my shoulder. "I suppose she figured I wouldn't stop searching for answers until I got to the truth."

"She was right, then." Mum held out the sceptre towards me. I hesitated for a moment before taking it from her, and the jewel embedded in its top began to glow as soon as my fingers closed around the end. Not a dream, then.

I didn't quite dare meet Mum's eyes. I'd claimed her lifelong goal by total accident and done it in such a way that it'd be the talk of the town for a generation. I turned over the long, thin instrument in my hand, causing the light to dance off the wall. Tansy leapt after it like a cat chasing a torchlight, and I rolled my eyes at her. "So… does the entire town know?"

"Yes," Mum said. "Ramsey said the *Blue Moon* printed a story first thing this morning despite his efforts to tell them otherwise. My sister was the one who made the call to tell them the news."

I grunted. "Guess I can't blame her for that. I did screw up her plans to claim it for her own."

"From what I heard, it sounds like your grandmother was the one who kept her from taking the sceptre, not you," said Mum. "Besides, the sceptre chooses one person. It would have always picked you."

"I don't know about that." I watched the play of light on the wall, unable to fully grasp the reality that such a powerful object was mine. For the time being. "Don't forget I carried the sceptre in the ceremony too. It didn't pick anyone then."

Unless it'd been waiting for the question of Grandma's death to be solved. Had my involvement in capturing Stacy helped? Perhaps, but it didn't mean I was worthy of representing the town as the regional Head Witch, especially when I'd never even led a coven.

"Nobody truly understands the sceptre's magic," she said. "Not even us. The most we can do is wield it the best we can."

I lowered my head. "You think I'm going to be the worst Head Witch in the town's history, don't you?"

"Only if *you* think that," she said. "And I don't think so at all. Clearly, the sceptre chose you for a reason."

"And it's only for a year." A year seemed a long time

away, but it'd go by in a flash, and besides, I couldn't think further ahead than tomorrow at the moment.

Mum backed out of my room. "Today, you're free to do as you wish before starting your new job tomorrow. I for one am curious to know if my mother intends to show her face again."

As she closed the door behind her, I picked up my phone and checked the Wizarding Web. The top story of the day bore the headline, *Wildwood Heath is in shock as the disgraced granddaughter of former Head Witch claims title.*

I muttered a curse under my breath and climbed out of bed. Aunt Shannon had spared no details in her call to the press, but my immediate family knew the truth, while Stacy was behind bars where she belonged. Grandma's ghost must have drifted off at some point, but I had an inkling she wouldn't be going quietly into the afterworld.

I had until tomorrow to come to grips with the idea of being the new Head Witch. Better get started.

Firstly, I took a long, hot shower and got dressed into my comfiest hoody and jeans. I debated for a moment before taking the sceptre downstairs with me, where I found Mum in the kitchen. "Is there somewhere safe I can store this? I shouldn't be carrying it around in public."

"Nobody can steal it from you, Robin," she said. "But you can feel free to leave it here with me if you want to go out without drawing attention."

"Thanks," I said, surprised. Mum seemed refreshed after her long sleep, almost… mild. Maybe Grandma had had the right idea. So had Carmilla, who lay curled up asleep in front of the fireplace and didn't stir. I wasn't sure if she did intend to keep an eye on me when I took

Grandma's place, but there ought to be one person in the Head Witch's office who knew what she was doing.

Pushing the thought aside, I called my dad on my way out of the house.

He answered at once. "Robin? Want to come over?"

"Are Jess and the kids there?"

"No, she took them out to the park for the day," he replied. "I figured I should stay here in case you needed to see me."

Gratitude welled within me. "It's appreciated."

I made my way along the woodland path. When I reached the cottage, he was already waiting outside. "Hey, Head Witch."

I groaned. "Don't even. It was an accident."

"I know." He pulled me into a hug. "I know this isn't what you wanted. Is your mother…"

"She seems fine." I followed him into the house. "Weirdly enough. Not sure if she's in shock or if she's just relieved that it isn't her sister who got the position. Though I'd bet she wants to keep a close watch on me."

Admittedly, she hadn't given that impression, but it was early days, and she must have assumed I'd be staying in my old room.

"You have authority over her now, don't you?" he asked. "You can tell her to give you space if you think she's getting too stifling."

I cringed. "She runs the coven, but the Head Witch… their main role is ceremonial, mostly. We're equals."

"It seems bizarre that someone can be chosen for the role without any warning," he commented. "Not that you aren't an accomplished witch—I heard what you did to catch your grandmother's killer—but you should at least have the choice."

I shook my head. "In another town, a kid got chosen as Head Witch, but she still had to take the job. All they could do was try to make sure her duties didn't interfere with her schoolwork. I have no idea how my boss is going to react when I tell him."

"You're allowed to keep your job?"

"I have no idea." I still hadn't the faintest idea what I was going to do about my life outside of Wildwood Heath. I had bills to pay, deliveries on the schedule, and yet I was expected to start another job entirely tomorrow morning. How was I supposed to explain that to anyone? "I bet the council will be keen to tell me that a Head Witch shouldn't be doing something as mundane as delivering packages to snooty wizards for a living."

"Do you enjoy your job?"

"It was supposed to be temporary," I admitted. "I was hoping for a promotion, but being chosen as Head Witch definitely isn't what I had in mind."

"It'd look great on your applications to any future jobs, though," he said.

"Guess you're right." I attempted a smile. "Hey, I have guaranteed employment for a year. Or until Samhain, anyway."

"Until..." he said. "That's right, I forgot your grand-mother was an anomaly. The sceptre picks a new wielder annually."

"Every Samhain." My smile faded. "If I do a terrible job, then it'll pick someone else next time."

"You won't."

"Mum said the same, if you can believe it," I said.

"Grandma… well, she laughed and said she'd rather I took her place than Aunt Shannon."

"You'll do fine," he said. "A few months is nothing, trust me. I wouldn't object to seeing you around more often."

"True." I just wished it hadn't come at the cost of my peace of mind. On the other hand, I'd inherited enough of the family stubbornness to want to give it my best shot, and besides, I kind of wanted to do a good job to spite everyone who said I couldn't. "I'll need somewhere to hide out from Aunt Shannon and Vanessa. They're livid at missing out to someone they feel doesn't deserve it."

"You do deserve it," he said. "It might not be what you wanted, but you earned that position. Don't doubt it for a second."

I smiled, this time for real, and my phone buzzed with a message.

Dad raised a brow. "I take it your friends want to see you?"

"Yeah." Actually, it was Harvey… and he'd asked if I wanted him to bring me coffee again on his way to his Sky Hopper practise session. That made my day infinitely better. "I need to tell them the news before the press gets there first."

"Don't let them get you down." He hugged me good-bye, and I left the cottage in a better mood than before. Even as Head Witch, I had one place to hide from the attention.

Famous last words. I came to a halt on the woodland path when I spotted two bright-crimson hats sticking up out of the bushes. Maybe I should have brought the sceptre out with me after all.

"Robin!" Clarice bounded to her feet, microphone in hand. "Do you want to do your first exclusive interview with us as Head Witch?"

"No thanks," I said. "What are you doing near my dad's house? Hoping to get an interview out of him too?"

She gave the cottage a hopeful look. "Would he do that for us?"

"Certainly *not*," I said. "Do you people have nothing better to do with your time than harass my family members?"

"It's you we want to speak to," Speck insisted. "If you just give us a few words on your thoughts on being chosen as Head Witch."

"Oh, I will."

"Really?" Clarice held out the microphone, her expression eager and bright.

"Get stuffed," I told her. "You've spent decades telling lies about my family. Grandma might have been lenient on you, but my first act as Head Witch is to ban you from ever coming near the Wildwood again."

Clarice's face fell. I took a step back, and a muttered instruction sent a wave of birds flying out of the nearby trees. With a shriek, Clarice and Speck fled down the path and out of sight.

With a rush of satisfaction, I walked back towards home and met Harvey in the same spot as before. Like last time, he held a latte in each hand.

"So it's true?" He handed me one of the lattes. "You really claimed the sceptre?"

"Yeah, lucky me." I blew on my drink to cool it down. "You didn't happen to see a couple of reporters, did you?"

"Were they dressed in red and running like a pack of wolves were chasing them?"

"That's them," I said. "I banned the press from the forest. Maybe I should have banned them from the coffee shop while I was at it, but even the Head Witch can't do that."

"You scared them pretty good," he commented. "Want me to chase them on my broom when I'm at practise later?"

"If the birds didn't give them a hint." I sipped my latte. "Thanks for this."

"If it's any consolation, I didn't see any press hanging around the coffee shop this time," he said. "Maybe we can go and get coffee there another time."

My heart skipped a beat. Was he asking me out? "Really?"

"Don't think I'm asking because of the Head Witch thing," he added. "I was always planning to anyway, and if you're going to be around here more often…"

I grinned. "Yes, I am. And yes, I'd like to."

"Good." He smiled, but his expression held a sense of hesitancy. "You didn't want to stay, though, did you?"

"Part of me did." My magic was tied to the Wildwood, after all. "I think it'll be different now."

I hoped it would be, anyway.

"Good," he said. "Your family… how did they take the news?"

"My aunt and cousin are furious, but they'll have to accept the sceptre's choice if they want to stay in the coven," I said. "My mum actually does seem okay with it. Maybe because she'd rather deal with me as Head Witch than have to take orders from my aunt. Not sure about my brother yet. He was too busy arresting the murderer."

"I bet," he said. "What happened to your grandmother's ghost?"

"She's still around," I said. "She's not supposed to stay long term, but we all figured she'll move on of her own accord." Besides, if I did take the job, I might need to ask for her advice.

"I hope so," he said. "I have to head to practise now, but when you want that coffee date, let me know."

"I have to start my new job tomorrow, so I'm not sure when I'll be free, but I'll let you know." I had to tie up a few loose ends first. Like notifying my current employer.

"Sure, no pressure." He smiled at me as we parted ways, while I tried to figure out how to break the news to my boss over the phone.

I reached Mum's house via the back route and spotted Tansy chasing pigeons in the garden. Behind her, Piper was hard at work trimming the roses.

I approached Piper at a fast stride. "You're back?"

"Yeah, your mum let me back in," she said. "Good job she did too. She's definitely not a garden witch... don't tell her I said that."

"I'm sure she'd agree." I hesitated for a second. "You heard?"

"Obviously," she said. "For the record, I support you."

"You don't think I'll do a bad job?" Despite my newfound resolve to make the best of the situation I'd landed in, I had zero idea what to expect. I might have grown up in the same house as a Head Witch, but there was a world of difference between that and having to actually do it myself. The sceptre had chosen me because

I'd solved the previous holder's murder, but its support might not extend beyond that.

"Of course I don't," she said. "Isn't it just a lot of sitting around doing paperwork and attending meetings?"

"Neither of those things is exactly a strong point of mine."

"Your grandmother had her assistant handle most of it," she said. "That's an option."

"I'd rather not give anyone a chance to poison me, thanks. Nearly getting crushed by a branch was bad enough on its own."

"I won't let anyone poison you," said Tansy. "Including certain *spiders.*"

I spun around, spotting Rowan watching me from the other side of the fence. My cousin jumped when Tansy spoke, her familiar climbing up her arm. "Hey, Robin."

Piper rose to her feet. "So you're the tattletale."

"I'm not—" Rowan broke off. "I'm sorry."

I didn't yet know whether I wanted to forgive her for what she'd done, not with the aftermath too raw. "For what, exactly? Telling tales to the press, betraying the coven, or summoning Grandma's ghost?"

"I... I summoned Grandma because I was worried my mum would claim the sceptre," she mumbled. "She was trying every method of cheating in the book to get as many votes for coven leader as possible, and I panicked. It wasn't just because of Tiffany. I had to stop her."

"You weren't anywhere to be seen when she actually *did* try to take the sceptre." If she had been, she might have claimed it herself and freed herself of being in her mother's shadow in the process. "And you let Tiffany push you around the same way she did. Joining the Henbane Coven won't solve any of your problems."

"I'm not joining the Henbane Coven," she said. "I pretended I was considering it in order to get Tiffany's protection, and she wanted me to help her get the sceptre. I'd rather have had her in charge than my mother, to be honest."

"You had no faith in the rest of us to help you. Even me."

"I didn't know you'd take the sceptre yourself!" she said. "I didn't think you even wanted it."

"I didn't intend to take it," I said. "If you'd been around to help me, I wouldn't have had to, either."

She blinked, tears shimmering in her eyes. "I'm not strong like you are. I couldn't have stopped her."

"You have got to get out of that house." One thing was clear: Aunt Shannon had crossed a line. Several of them. "I'm not going to say I don't understand why you did it, but you can't let her control your life."

"I won't." She drew in a breath. "You should know… Grandma came to visit me earlier. She said she left me some money in her will."

"She visited you?"

She inclined her head. "My mum was raging mad when she came home, but Grandma showed up and scared her before she could start berating me. She terrified Vanessa too."

"Good," I said. "So you're moving out?"

She didn't have much choice. Aunt Shannon had been cruel enough to her before she'd thought she had a shot at the title of Head Witch, and I didn't want to imagine how much worse she'd get now that she'd lost her chance.

"The nice guys at Were's My Coffee? have a spare flat upstairs and offered to let me move in tomorrow," she said. "I just wanted to tell you that I never wanted you dead. Or Grandma either. It wasn't me."

"I know you didn't," I said. "I never wanted to think you did."

Piper glowered at her. "But you're still a coward."

"Never said I wasn't." Rowan glanced over at her house. "Ah, I don't think my mum is plotting to take the sceptre away from you or anything."

Yet. It'd only been a day, and it sounded as though Grandma had kept her busy with her ghostly distractions. "It's not like she doesn't get a second chance at the sceptre in October."

Rowan shuddered. "Don't say that."

"It's true," said Piper. "I hope for all our sakes that you pick the right person to back next time around."

Namely my mother. Mum deserved the sceptre more than I did, but it wouldn't hurt to have the chance to lord it over Aunt Shannon for a bit before then. "You'd better hurry up and move your stuff to your new place before Aunt Shannon figures out what you did."

"Oh, I know." She flashed me a quick smile. "I'll see you later."

"I'd keep an eye on her," Piper muttered to me when she disappeared. "Her loyalties are pretty suspect."

"Look at the rest of her immediate family, though." I watched Tansy tussle with a pigeon over the bird feeder for a moment before I spotted Ramsey approaching us.

"Robin." He came to a halt next to the rosebushes. "There you are."

"Ramsey," I said. "You're not at work?"

"No, but I went to make sure they had Stacy secured anyway," he said. "Does the Head Witch need any help with preparing for tomorrow?"

"Please don't talk about me in the third person," I said. "It's weird."

Piper snickered. "Yes, it is. What would she need your help with, anyway?"

He fiddled with his coat sleeve. "Can I talk to you alone, Robin?"

"Sure, why not." I beckoned to Tansy, who scurried down the bird feeder and joined me. "What is it?"

"To start off with, I wanted to apologise for suspecting you of talking to the press."

I raised a brow. "Does it have anything to do with you being scared I'll smite you with the sceptre if you annoy me?"

"No," he said. "I screwed up. Clearly, you're worthy of being chosen."

"Thanks. I think." I gave him a sideways look. "You know I wouldn't actually smite you, don't you?"

"She would," Tansy helpfully said. "And I'd watch and laugh."

"She's joking," I said. When he kept staring at me, I said, "What?"

"Someone tried to have you killed," he said. "I thought it wise to set up some new security spells on your office, but I need your approval first."

I groaned inwardly. "This is supposed to be my day off."

"Do you want to give your potential killers a chance to put a deadly curse on your office?"

"Seriously?" He hadn't wasted any time in jumping to

the worst conclusions. "I'd be impressed if they managed to come up with a deadly curse that quickly, but fine, I'll come and check on your spells."

"Good." His expression relaxed minutely. "This is a dangerous job. You—"

"I know the risks, and I don't need a lecture," I interjected. "I did actually live here for most of my life, you know. Just because I haven't been around the last few years doesn't mean I don't remember."

"Of course not." But he kept up a steady stream of redundant tips as we headed to the coven headquarters, while I nodded and pretended to listen. Of course I was a little concerned about potential murder attempts, but it would have been nice to get one day to myself. I hadn't even learned to use the sceptre yet.

As we entered the coven's headquarters, Ramsey paused in his tirade for long enough to say, "You'll also have to redo the wards on the office door so you and Mum are the only people who can enter."

"Maybe later." I headed mechanically to the office… *my* office. Given the state it'd been in yesterday, I was not looking forward to tidying up.

When I opened the door, however, it was to find the room restored to its usual orderly state, with the cabinets closed and the desk returned to the centre of the room. A shiny camera lay in the centre of the wooden surface. "Is that what I think it is?"

"I went out and got it this morning."

I don't know which of us was more surprised when I hugged him with a squeal of delight. "Oh, my god, Ramsey."

"No need for that," he said gruffly.

I released him. "I—thought Mum had forgotten all about this, to be honest. I figured a sceptre is enough of a reward."

If you could call it that. I had the sinking suspicion that I'd won my family's respect at the cost of my freedom.

Ramsey made a startled noise. "Grandma."

My attention snapped up. Grandma's ghost stood in the corner of the office, and when she saw me looking, she gave me a wave. "Are you ready for tomorrow?"

"I will be." I drew in a breath. "Bring it on."

ABOUT THE AUTHOR

Elle Adams lives in the middle of England, where she spends most of her time reading an ever-growing mountain of books, planning her next adventure, or writing. Elle's books are humorous mysteries with a paranormal twist, packed with magical mayhem.

She also writes urban and contemporary fantasy novels as Emma L. Adams.

Visit http://www.elleadamsauthor.com/ to find out more about Elle's books.